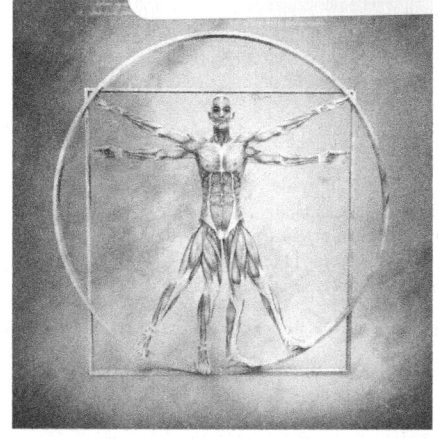

The Human Chronicles Saga

Book One:

The Fringe Worlds

By

T.R. Harris

Published by

Harris Publications

Copyright 2011 by T.R. Harris

ISBN: 978-0-9858849-8-7

All rights reserved, without limiting the rights under copyright reserved above, no part of this publication may be reproduced, stored in or introduced into a retrieval system, or transmitted, in any form, or by any means (electronic, mechanically, photocopying, recording, or otherwise) without the prior written permission of both the copyright owner and the above publisher of this book. This is a work of fiction. Names, characters, places, brands, media and incidents are either the product of the author's imagination or are used fictitiously.

■■■

Go to **TheHumanChronicles.com** for more information about the series and to help contribute to future volumes.

Contact author **T.R. Harris** directly at
bytrharris@hotmail.com
He welcomes all comments, critiques and suggestions.

Pick up all the books in
The Human Chronicles Saga

The Human Chronicles Saga: Part One – 5 Books

Book 1 – *The Fringe Worlds*

Book 2 – *Alien Assassin*

Book 3 – *The War of Pawns*

Book 4 – *The Tactics of Revenge*

Book 5 – *The Legend of Earth*

The Human Chronicles Saga: Part Two

Book 1 – *Cain's Crusaders*

See the back of this book for a Special Preview of

Alien Assassin

Book 2
The Human Chronicles Saga

****

What other readers are saying about

The Fringe Worlds...

This book is just plain fun. It's a light, easy and fast read; it doesn't mess around or waste words; and it doesn't pretend to be anything that it's not. It's just a throw-down space fighting, barroom brawling, shoot-em up, tough-guys in the galaxy tale that anyone with a sense of humor and a love of sci-fi in the flavor of Douglas Adams will enjoy. — **John Daulton, author of The Galactic Mage Series**

One of the best SF books I've read in a long time! Harris gives a concise story, efficient adventure and characters I cheered for! I can hardly wait for the next installment! — **Genie233**

A truly amazing piece of sci-fi literature that only has one flaw - once you start reading it, you cannot put it down, and that will make you reach the end of it rather soon. The story is extremely easy to read, amusing and leaves you hungry for the sequel. Read it if you look for entertainment that makes you feel better about yourself as a human. One of the best reads in the field of sci-fi that I have come across for years! — **Urmas**

The Fringe Worlds

by

T.R. Harris

Adam Cain is an alien with an attitude. Here's the reason why...

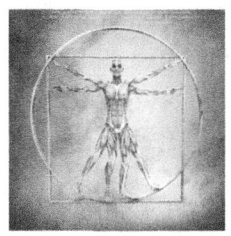

Chapter 1

W__hoever designed this ship should be shot!__
After all, with focusing rings so crucial to the operation of the gravity drive, Kaylor never figured out why the designers had set them in the most difficult areas of the ship to reach—*and this ring was for the main generator.*

Annoyed, Kaylor felt another bead of sweat flow down his forehead and into his left eye. Cursing under his breath, he tried to regain focus in the eye, while adjusting the gripper unit for yet another stab at the focusing ring. Normally, fitting the ring back into its cradle wouldn't have been such a chore, but the tool he was using was old and the gears kept slipping, allowing the ring to wobble. It was like this for just about everything else aboard his ship these days, and like the gripper unit, changes and updates were long overdue.

In reality, Kaylor couldn't complain too much about the condition of his ship, not considering the price he'd paid for her. The *FS-475* was an old cargo hauler, and he had come upon her drifting out beyond the Silean Sector of The Void after having been attacked and stripped by the Fringe Pirates. He never learned the fate of the crew, content in the knowledge that the vastness of space was a very convenient place to hide the bodies....

After the salvage had been awarded, it had taken him over three years to piece together enough spare parts to make her space-worthy again. Then with an operational ship he could call his own, Kaylor had confidently entered the office of his current hauler boss, carrying with him a well-rehearsed plan for a substantial increase in his commission rate.

Unfortunately, the meeting didn't go exactly as planned.

He'd entered the meeting as a senior pilot for a very large and well-connected shipping operation. He left as a *freelance* mule-driver with no contracts to speak of and all his savings tied up in the repair of the *FS-475*. But that had been fourteen standard years ago, and even though most of the intervening years consisted of barely subsistence wages, Kaylor had survived, if not living out his dream of fame and fortune among the stars, then at least managing to make ends meet.

Now if I could just get this finicky gripper onto the ring....

With his body contorted in the narrow access tube like some Castorian string dancer, all he had to do now was get the gripper unit up and over a protruding electrical conduit and around a blind ninety-degree bend in the access tube—and do it all by feel. So he reached forward once again, both arms outstretched to their max, carefully, until he felt the unit contact the ring. Then with a push of the control button on the gripper's handle, he heard the click of victory as the unit finally gained control of the focusing ring. Then with another press of the button, he heard the welcoming whirl as the ring was tightened back into place.

Exhausted, Kaylor collapsed on the hard metal surface and closed his eyes, his breathing labored and amplified by the walls of the tube.

What an ordeal.

A recalibration hadn't really been necessary, not with the ring out of focus by less than half a degree. But he'd decided to do it anyway, as a foolish attempt to escape the excruciating and mind-numbing boredom that came with transiting The Void. That was three hours ago. Now exhausted and soaked in sweat, he lie in the dim, confined space of the third-level access tube thinking about what an incredible waste of time this had been, and lamenting on all the other bad decisions he'd made throughout his life.

His quiet revere was interrupted when a phantom voice echoed around him. "Kaylor, you better get down here."

"What is it, Jym?"

"I have a contact."

His heart skipped a beat as he was hit with the ramifications of those four innocent words. Without hesitation, Kaylor scooped up his tool kit and began shimming down the access tube. "I'm on my way."

It was only a short distance down the generator corridor to the second level access ladder, yet it was time enough for Kaylor to conjure up any number of dire scenarios for the news he'd just received. To be in the vicinity of another ship this far into The Void was almost unheard of; the odds were way beyond coincidence. And without the possibility of assistance from any planetary authority, it also meant that the two of them were on their own against whatever threat this contact may pose.

Sliding quickly down the ladder, Kaylor half-sprinted the remaining distance to the open doorway of the pilothouse. Entering, he slipped in past Jym seated at the nav console, engrossed in his calculations, and fell into the driver's seat. On the screen before him was a bright blip of light in the upper right corner, moving slowly at a diagonal toward the center of the screen. The blip was extremely bright, indicating that the ship was either very large or at max-drive. Either way, the contact was a threat.

"Any indication he sees us?" Kaylor asked.

"None; we've been dark since you've been working on the generators."

Fortunate for us, Kaylor thought. Maybe something good actually did come out of his ordeal with the focusing ring. The only energy signatures they would be giving off would be from the ship's own gravity wells, which were too weak to be detected this far out. Kaylor began to relax a little, as he watched the distance between the contact and his ship increase inexorable from the momentum they still carried, even without the generators fired up. This just might be okay—

Just then the large blip separated into two smaller ones and began to expand into a shallow "V" formation. Simultaneously, Kaylor and Jym leaned in closer to their screens, looking for any indication of hostile intent. With none coming, they shared a collective sigh of relief.

"How long until we're out of range?" Kaylor asked, not taking his eyes from the screen.

Jym tapped some keys on the nav console. "In about half an hour." He then slipped out of his seat and headed for the doorway. "How about some Hildorian tea while we wait?"

"Sounds good, I'll keep watch." At least Jym seemed relaxed enough to accept the situation. Yet knowing the emotional tendencies of his co-pilot, Kaylor suspected Jym had the intention of dropping a little blue pill into his tea. Maybe Kaylor should follow suit....

Nearly half an hour later, Kaylor and Jym sat with their feet up on their consoles, sipping tea and enjoying the light narcotic effects of the intoxicants. The two contacts were now very close to the right edge of the view screen and in a few more minutes they would be out of range. Kaylor would then fire up the generators and bolt out of the area. It was only then that he would fully let down his guard.

Suddenly, the two blips flared bright—*and disappeared from the screen!*

In unison, Kaylor and Jym dove for their consoles, Kaylor spilling the tea down the front of his tunic in the process. Ignoring the hot liquid, he began to prep the generators for power.

"Do you have them?" he barked out.

"I'm working on it." Jym was feverishly tapping the keys of his console as two flashing red circles appeared on the screen where the contacts had last been indicated. "From the strength of the back-wells, it looks like they've come to a stop," Jym said incredulously.

"They didn't change course with the back-well?"

"It doesn't look like it. They've gone dark ... and are just sitting out there."

"That doesn't make any sense." Kaylor continued his preparations, yet resisted activating the generators, a move which would clearly announce their presence. Taking a chance that they could still slip out of range undetected, he waited. *Just a few more minutes. Still, why would—*

Kaylor stopped in mid-thought as another blip appeared on the screen, this one carrying a massive gravity signature and entering out of the upper left corner of the screen. Kaylor glanced over at Jym, who stared back at him, his mouth half-opened. He simply shrugged, answering the silent question.

Then it all began to make sense, as yet another, smaller contact appeared on the screen, following closely behind the massive blip, in obviously pursuit. Kaylor didn't need to comment. Both of them knew what was happening: *Pirates!*

"But there are three of them," Jym announced to the room. "I've never heard of that many pirates working together before."

"This is true, but look at the signature of that ship. It's incredible!" A few taps of his board and Kaylor had his answer. "They're at 98% efficiency." His ship operated at 75%, max. "Those generators would be worth a fortune."

"If the pirates can catch it," Jym countered, and by the ever-increasing gap between the large ship and its pursuer, it was obvious that wasn't going to happen.

"They don't have to catch it; they've already laid a pretty good trap." Kaylor was right. The pursuing ship was herding the large target straight for the two dark contacts. The outcome was inevitable, and in a few minutes the carnage would begin.

Fortunately for Kaylor and Jym they would not be around to see it, as their momentum was just about to carry them out of range—and to safety.

Yet Kaylor still felt a pang of disappointment. The gravity generators on that ship would have been something to see. He had never heard of 98% efficiency being achieved before. And besides the generators, what other treasures did a ship that advanced carry in her? Of course, Kaylor's question was rhetorical, since the outcome of the attack was a foregone conclusion. Three pirates, operating in concert, would be able to bring down a ship that size with relative ease. And then they would have all the time they needed to pick it clean….

Suddenly Kaylor sat straight up in his seat, his eyes wide and focused on the screen before him. Jym noticed the movement. "What's wrong?" he asked.

"I just got an idea."

"No, no you didn't." Jym didn't like the look on Kaylor's face.

"Yes, I did. And this will work!" He leaned forward and began programming the piloting computer. "Pull up the ship's inventory. I need to know if we still have those satellite drones on board."

"You're not thinking about doing what I'm thinking you're thinking about doing, are you?" The sentence was awkward, but accurate.

Kaylor swiveled his chair until he was facing Jym. "This is a-once-in-a-lifetime opportunity!" His voice was animated, his face alight with excitement.

Jym had seen this look before, and it made him nervous. "We can't take on three pirates. We're a muleship, with no weapons to speak of except for that pea-gun you installed last year. How do you propose we do this?"

"Remember a few years back, when we used a drone as a decoy to slip out of New Regian with those Regulators after us? We'll do that." He scanned the inventory list Jym had just posted on his screen. "We have six drones on board. We hook grapples on them, fan them out on either side of the ship and then set their front- and back-wells at maximum. To the pirates we'll look like a whole fleet of Rigorian warships, six of them, plus us in the middle. There's no way they'll want to take on seven warships."

"And then what, we just glide in and pick up the remains?" Jym still wasn't buying it. "What if there's still some crew left alive? You can't claim a salvage without a derelict."

Jym had a point. Kaylor hadn't figured on the pirates not completing their kill by the time he scared them off. "In that case, we should get a reward from the ship's owners," he offered. But that still wasn't good enough. Then softer, "Or we'll let the pirates have a little more time to dispose of the crew before we move in."

"Oh that's really civilized of us." Jym spat out sarcastically.

"We're not the pirates here, Jym!" Kaylor countered. He was getting mad. This was a tremendous opportunity—for both of them. One big score like this and they wouldn't have to keep towing cheap cargos back and forth throughout the Fringe. But Jym wasn't seeing it.

"And what if the pirates don't scare off? What do we do then?"

Kaylor turned back to his screen to finish the intercept calculations. Then half under his breath, he answered, "Then we'll bolt out. We're pretty fast—when we're not towing a string."

"You're going to dump the string!" Jym yelled back.

Kaylor had had enough. He turned to face Jym again. "Just prep the drones! And yes, we'll dump the string if we have to. We can always come back for it later. This salvage will be worth a hundred strings of smokesticks. Now I don't want to hear any more objections. Just do it!"

Although they had crewed together for a long time, and were more like brothers than shipmates, Jym knew Kaylor was the boss. Besides, he had been right more often than not. So with one last defiant sigh, Jym turned to his console and began prepping the drones.

"I hope this works," was all he said.

Me too, Kaylor thought. *Me too*.

It was simply called **The Void**, an impossibly empty region of space approximately forty-eight light years long and eighteen wide. Devoid of even the most basic nebulae, dwarf stars, rouge asteroids or comets, The Void had been vacuumed clean a billion years before by a wandering black hole, until now it existed as a literal desert in space.

Along its inner rim lay The Fringe, a cluster of some thirty-seven stars of various classifications and supporting twelve habitable planets, ranging from the heavy rock giant of K'ly to the wispy and gaseous Dimloe, with its four-meter tall inhabitants known for their grotesque cannibalistic rituals.

Along the outer edge of The Void lay the Barrier, a dense, diaphanous cloud of pre-stellar gas, aglow in brilliant hues of red, green and orange. Though beautiful to behold, the Barrier was just that, the defining line between the civilized galaxy that reached to the Core and beyond, and the Far Arm, with its untold millions of unexplored systems stretching all the way to the very edge of the galaxy. Unable to be pierced by conventional scanners or optical telescopes, much of what lie beyond the Barrier was nothing more than rumor, myth or supposition.

The Void restricted the outward migration of civilization into the Far Arm, keeping that region of space a mystery to all but the most daring or foolhardy.

Along this frontier territory of the Juirean Expansion was where the true galactic pioneers plied their craft, made up of merchants, miners and entrepreneurs, along with some of the most-vile criminals who had ever existed. Life in The Fringe Worlds was not easy, but for some, it was all they knew.

The Fringe was where Kaylor and Jym eked out their meager living, hauling strings of often forbidden cargo from one port to the next, staying mindful of the ever-changing political climate of each individual world in The Fringe.

Case in point: Silean Smokesticks. The Sileans prided themselves for the smoothness and strength of the herb that went into their 'sticks, which made them a valuable and cherished commodity to the Rigorians, who used them in many of their religious ceremonies—or so they claimed. If this were true, then the lizard-like Rigorians were some of the most religious beings in the galaxy, consuming smokesticks like candy. The problem was that to get from Silea to Rigor meant crossing Li'Polan space, where being caught selling any kind of intoxicant carried with it an uncontestable sentence of death.

So to avoid Li'Polan space, hard-working traders like Kaylor and Jym were often forced to endure a three-week-long transit of The

Void, having to go so far out of their way that after each trip Kaylor swore it would be his last. And yet 'sticks were worth a small fortune on Rigor....

Having prepped and deployed the drones, Kaylor pulled the *FS-475* far enough away from the range barrier so he could get a running start toward the pirates. The plan was to build up a pretty good head of steam, then go dark and coast in the rest of the way undetected. Then as they grew closer, he would fire up the wells and surprise the pirates. As Kaylor explained to a still-skeptical Jym, he didn't want the pirates to have too much time to build up the courage to confront his phantom fleet. By dropping in at the last minute, he was hoping for a spontaneous reaction and an instinctive flight to safety.

At the right moment, Kaylor dissolved the well and went dark.

At this range, they were too far out to see the pirates visually, but the overlapping circles on the view screen began to creep ever closer to the left edge of the screen. The timing would be a judgment call. If he fired up too soon, the pirates might have time to analyze their gravity signatures and see through his ruse, and if he waited too long, they might feel they have little choice but to stay and fight. So as the distance closed, and the tension in the pilothouse grew thicker, Kaylor began to have second thoughts about his entire plan....

In a few minutes they had closed to within extreme visual range and Kaylor and Jym got their first real look at their targets. In the center was a large disk-shaped ship, clearly ten times or more the size of the three oblong-shaped pirate ships surrounding it. One of the pirates had attached an umbilical to the large ship while the other two lay out at a distance, like wild beasts waiting patiently for their turn at the carcass.

There were burn marks along the hull of the target ship, with one prominent line running up and across a bulging pilot dome at the center of the disk. The ship had very few viewports along the fuselage, yet the ones that were present still had light shining from them. Kaylor tried to keep his imagination from conjuring up visions of what must be going on aboard the large ship. He knew pirates did not take prisoners; there was just no money in ransom in The Fringe since life here was so cheap. So it was only the hardware they were after. Soft-flesh creatures were just an obstacle to an end. And Kaylor was letting the killing go on for his own selfish goals. Oh well....

Finally, it was now or never. Either he was going to do this or not. About then, a strange calm descended over Kaylor—a resignation of sorts—and he engaged the wells.

The effect was almost instantaneous. Within a minute, the two outer pirate ships fired up their back-wells and streaked off in the opposite direction from Kaylor's line of approach. A few moments later, the umbilical tore away from the third pirate ship, and it began a wide sweep behind the large ship using its chemical drive.

But then the unexpected happened: The pirate ship continued its sweep, and ended up facing Kaylor and his phantom fleet, just sitting there.

"He's not leaving!" Jym shouted the obvious.

Kaylor stared so intently at the pirate ship on the screen that he felt he and the pirate captain were looking directly into each other's eyes, daring the other to act. Yet neither waivered.

As the seconds passed, Jym began to fidget, glancing from his screen, then to Kaylor and back again, repeatedly. And still Kaylor stared.

Finally Jym had had enough. He reached for his own pilot stick, determined to change course if Kaylor wouldn't—

Just then the pirate ship moved, and for an instant, they both stopped breathing, as the pirate came straight for them. Then at the last moment, the ship turned about, activated its gravity drive and bolted away in the opposite direction, disappearing visually as it sank into its own event horizon.

Kaylor and Jym let out simultaneous cries of victory—and relief.

Collapsing into his chair, Kaylor closed his eyes momentarily, the pounding of his heart seeming to drown out all other sounds around him. The ruse had worked, but barely. As he sat there, Kaylor tried to imagine what madness the pirate captain could have been thinking? He knew that three pirate ships, working in unison, was a formidable force, yet not against seven warships, even imaginary ones. Whoever that captain was, he was either a reckless fool or a ruthless bastard. Either way, that was way too close for Kaylor's liking.

The pirate ships were off-screen before Kaylor and Jym powered down and slipped in next to the stricken ship, but they knew they were still lurking in the area. Kaylor's immediate plan was to attach an umbilical of his own and go aboard the ship for a quick survey and to see if anyone was left alive, including any abandoned pirates. Then they would attach grapples to the big ship and pull it away before the pirates worked up the courage to come back. There would be plenty of time for salvage on the way to Nimor, where they would register the salvage and make it all official.

Jym opened the outer viewport shield so he and Kaylor could get their first look at the huge ship in natural light. The ship *was* huge, easily five or six times the mass of Kaylor's muleship, yet the configuration was all wrong. Very few ships were disk-shaped and it had only a few nodes interrupting the smoothness of its shiny hull. It was a beautiful ship, and Kaylor was literally salivating thinking of what riches it held inside.

And so it was with an almost childlike enthusiasm that Kaylor suited up and began the trek through the umbilical, and into what he had already began to refer to as his "retirement."

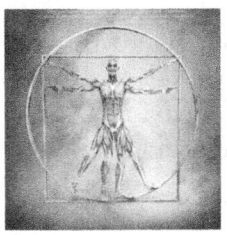

Chapter 2

Even though the scans indicated that there was an atmosphere and gravity aboard the ship, Kaylor nevertheless wore an environment suit as he crossed the umbilical. There was a working airlock on the other side, and once he was safely through, he raised the visor on his helmet and took in a deep gulp of air. There was a strong trace of ozone, along with the distinctive scent of burning flesh. Even though the smell was offensive, he keep the visor open so he could hear better, cautious of any threats that might still linger within the ship.

He found himself in a wide corridor that curved off in either direction following the gentle circumference of the ship. Proceeding carefully, he soon came upon two dead Jakreans, their gray flesh burned in several spots, gray tunics stained with blood. He wasn't surprised to find Jakreans aboard; after all, they were the workhorses of the galaxy; semi-intelligent beings who followed orders and had no imagination of their own. Kaylor was sure he'd find several more, just like these, during his survey.

Next he came upon a wide window set in the wall to his right. On the other side was a vast room lined with row upon row of what appeared to be hiberpods. He'd never seen so many pods in one room. Curious, he entered the room through an open doorway and found three more dead Jakreans, along with another being, this one taller and dressed all in silver. Its head was large, with a long sloping forehead and a crest of long white hair. The creature had been shot in the back and had fallen on its side. Red blood pooled under the creature, and there was a laser weapon still in the dead grasp of the creature. *Looks like he at least tried to put up a fight....*

Moving closer to the pods, Kaylor noticed that they were all occupied by creatures still hooked to the fluid tubes, yet oddly, each one he could see had a small, bloody puncture wound at its temple.

All the canopies on the pods were open and a quick count of the rows put the total pods at eighty. Moving quickly past the dead silver creature, Kaylor confirmed that each of the creatures in the pods had the same wound to their temples—the distinctive type of wound indicative of a laser weapon, such as the one held by the dead silver being.

All the creatures in the pods had been executed.

But that didn't make any sense; the creatures in the pods were all primes, mostly male, well-muscled and about average height. Kaylor didn't recognize the species, but that wasn't unusual. With over eight-thousand known primes in the Juirean Expansion, he wasn't expected to be up on every one of them. Yet these creatures had been intentionally killed, and not by the pirates, but rather by the apparent owners of the ship.

"Are you seeing this?" Kaylor asked through his comm-unit.

Jym answered immediately. "This is strange. Those hiberpods are some of the most advanced and expensive I've ever seen. You do not transport just anyone in them, and then turn around and kill them all. But you better get moving, Kaylor. The pirates won't stay gone for long."

Jym was right. Once they got the grapples on and slipped into a well, he'd have plenty of time to come back for a more thorough accounting.

He left the pod room and proceeded further down the corridor, passing three more dead Jakreans and two more of the silver creatures. Everything was silent. There was no indication that anyone else was aboard the ship—at least no one left alive.

After a while, Kaylor came upon a wide stairway on his left leading toward the center of the ship. Logically, this would lead to the bridge.

The command center was situated in the central dome area he'd seen from outside. All the control consoles were located along the outer wall, and opposite them was a large central bank of equipment modules and computers towering about twelve feet high. Kaylor could clearly see where one of the blasts from the pirates' flash weapons had penetrated the command dome, slashing through a section of the consoles before being contained by sealing foam. The room was airtight now, and even some of the electronics still functioned.

He moved to one of the consoles and began a quick survey of the control units he could see. They were magnificent, some of the most sophisticated he'd ever seen. Then turning his attention to the equipment bank behind him, Kaylor was equally impressed by the navigation and life support units he saw. This was the mother lode. Not only were there salvageable units here, but they were also probably the most-expensive he'd ever seen. And he hadn't even been to the generator room yet.

And there was the *computer core*—the single-most valuable piece of equipment aboard the ship—besides the massive gravity generators. The cores of interstellar command computers were some of the most-sophisticated pieces of equipment to be found anywhere, and with a thriving black market adept at reprogramming them for subsequent resale at astounding rates. Normally, the core would have been the first treasure removed from the ship; it was a miracle that this one was still here. And unlike the bulky and impossible-to-remove gravity generators, the core was something he could easily haul back to his ship.

Moving to the equipment bank, Kaylor flicked the four securing latches at each corner of the three-foot-square module. He grabbed the two side handles of the core and pulled the unit from its rack. Instantly, he noticed that the three steady orange lights in the equipment bank above the core suddenly turned yellow and began to oscillate from right to left. Before he could ponder why, he was interrupted—

"Kaylor!" It was Jym on the comm-unit.

"Yes, I know, I better hurry up—"

"No, that's not it."

"Pirates?"

"No. You're not going to believe this, but I'm picking up gamma signatures."

Kaylor was stunned by the comment. "Strong?"

"Yes. I think the source is right there in the room with you."

Kaylor couldn't believe what he was hearing. "Why would they have a nuclear device onboard?"

"It could be a self-destruct of some kind," Jym offered.

"Can you pin-point the source?" Having let the computer core fall to the deck with a metal-on-metal thud, Kaylor frantically scanned the room, looking for any kind of unit that looked like a self-destruct control. Seeing none, he was about grab the core and head for the exit when Jym spoke again.

"The source is about four feet in front of you, somewhere in the equipment bank. And Kaylor, the signal's getting stronger."

Directly in front of him was the recess opening left by the computer's central core. Bending down, Kaylor inserted himself into the gap and turned on his helmet light. In the back of the recess he spotted a rectangular box with a control panel and a lighted display. And on the display was a counter, methodically clicking down numbers...

Kaylor knew Jym could see this, too. "What do you know about this?"

"I'll run it through the Library." In a moment Jym's voice came back on the line. "It's a self-destruct all right. A timer is counting down—at zero, we're nothing but a radioactive cloud."

"How long do we have? Can we get out of range in time?" Kaylor gritted his teeth in anger. He was so close to the big score, and now it looked as though he'd have to abandon the salvage.

"Oh no!" Jym screamed in his ear.

"What's wrong?"

"At the pace of the countdown, the device will activate in less than seven minutes."

Kaylor was stunned. It would take him at least five minutes just to get back to his ship. Even Jym would need at least seven minutes or more just to charge up the generators to get away on his own. Escape seemed impossible.

As the sense of resignation once again descended on Kaylor, he simply stated, "Then we'll have to disarm it."

There was a moment's silence on the comm-line before Jym came back on. "I'm scanning to see if there are any instructions in the Library for disarming such a device. Give me a moment."

"A moment's all we have."

Less than thirty seconds later, Jym came back on the line. "I've got something. The controls appear to be a simple degradation program. It says that if we can reverse the contacts, the process should be reversed, adding time instead of subtracting it."

Could it really be that simple? Kaylor didn't ponder the question long. Instead he inserted himself further into the opening until he was only inches from the control panel. Then pulling a small tool kit from a utility pocket in his environment suit, he took out a motorized screw extractor and set to work removing the outer panel to the timing device. The work went quickly, and soon he was looking into the guts of the control unit. There were wires and connectors and several circuit boards. "Which one is the timer?"

"It says to follow the leads from the display panel."

"It's right here in front."

Taking at gripping tool from the kit, Kaylor reached into the unit, past the maze of wires and to the circuit board beyond. Positioning the gripper, he was just about to lock down on the board when he suddenly felt a painful clamping on both of his ankles—and he was violently yanked out of the opening!

He flew across the room, landing hard on top of the command console, shocked and dazed, his ribs burning. As he regained his senses, Kaylor found he was face-to-face with one of the primes from the hiberpods, naked except for a sheet wrapped around its lower torso. But this creature definitely was not dead. Instead, it glared at him, clinching its fists and baring its teeth in a sign of open challenge.

And then it charged!

Raising his arm in defense, Kaylor did so just in time to block the strike from the insane creature. Instantly, Kaylor let out a high-pitched scream, as he felt his arm break from the incredible impact. Intense fire-like pain coursed through his arm, before the suit could inject a pain killer, bringing with it at least a bearable degree of relief.

But the creature wasn't done. The crazed beast grabbed Kaylor by his environment suit and threw him off the console, sending him once again flying across the room. Even is his pain-filled stupor, Kaylor was amazed at the strength this creature exhibited!

Landing hard on the floor with another spasm of pain, this time in his right shoulder, Kaylor rolled to his right and managed to pull his MK-17 as he did so. He pointed it at his attacker, who hesitated, staring at the weapon. But when no bolt came forth, the creature pounced again.

Just in time, the targeting computer locked onto his attacker, and Kaylor depressed the trigger. A ball of blue lightening flashed out of the barrel, striking the creature directly in the chest. The alien was thrown back against the control console, screaming in pain—but it didn't go down. Instead, the insane beast swatted at its chest and at the already-blistering skin and burned hair. The creature was stunned, but only momentarily.

Kaylor was shocked that the creature was still alive, but his shock soon turned to terror as his assailant pushed off from the console and leapt in the air toward—

Just then, Kaylor's stomach rose up in his mouth and he nearly vomited, as the gravity wells for the ship dissolved, leaving Kaylor—and his attacker—weightless and disoriented.

The charging creature was caught unprepared. The sudden loss of gravity caused it to remain airborne in its flight—and it soared directly over Kaylor; even as it passed overhead, the beast still tried to reach down and grab him. But it missed by a hair, and with its head turned back toward Kaylor, the creature slammed into the opposite wall with a dull thud, striking a sharp protrusion on the bulkhead. Instantly, the wild beast went limp, as small droplets of blood began to fill the air around the drifting body.

Kaylor lay on the deck, bruised, battered and in shock, the medicine from the suit fighting a losing battle against the pain of his shattered arm. In the zero gravity, he began to drift upward slightly, until the magnets in his boots activated and he found himself in an upright position.

He became aware of the screaming in his helmet. It was Jym.

"I'm...I'm all right," he said unsurely.

"The BOMB, Kaylor! Hurry!"

The bomb? *THE BOMB!*

Regaining his senses, Kaylor ignored the pain in his broken arm the best he could and dove for the computer core opening. The timer was down to 94-93-92. Looking around, Kaylor found the gripper tool now floating near the top of the opening. Grabbing it with his good right hand, he quickly positioned it onto the circuit board and pulled.

The board did not move. It would not come out!

"Try again!" Jym screamed.

With only one good arm, Kaylor did his best to reposition the gripper more to the center of the board and pulled again. This time it popped out. Kaylor quickly turned the board around, letting it cycle through the zero-gravity before grabbing the gripper once again with his good hand, Three times in rapid succession Kaylor tried unsuccessfully to place the board back into the slot, then on the fourth try, success.

Instantly, the counter—which by now was down to 16—began to click upwards. 17-18-19.

Kaylor was in too much pain to celebrate his victory. His ribs burned, his broken arm screamed with pain and his right shoulder throbbed in time with his rapidly beating heart.

"Are we going to live?" asked Jym's equally exhausted voice.

"For a little while longer, I'm afraid."

A few moments later it was time to get back to work. Extracting himself from the recess opening, Kaylor spotted the still-unconscious creature drifting near the ceiling to his right. The blood bubbles hadn't grown more numerous, so the wound must have sealed itself, and from the slow, rhythmic movements of the creature's chest, Kaylor could tell it was still alive.

Making a decision he hoped he wouldn't live to regret, Kaylor pulled a connecting cord from his suit and fastened one end of it to a corner latch on the computer core. Then reaching up with his right arm, he grasped a bare foot of the creature, and began to move toward the exit, trailing the core and the creature behind him like a pair of bizarre, mismatched balloons.

"Set the grapples, Jym," he commanded. "I'm on my way back."

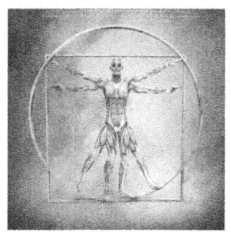

Chapter 3

Within the hour, Kaylor and Jym were back in a well, half a million kilometers away from the location of the attack, and with the large derelict ship in tow. Kaylor found Jym in the aft cargo hold, cinching down the last of five cargo straps around the still-unconscious creature, now firmly secured to one of the work benches in the room. Jym wasn't taking any chances; he'd seen what this thing could do.

Kaylor wore a blue cast encasing his broken left arm and had placed a torso brace around his bruised ribs for support and comfort. The pain medication was helping, but still his arm throbbed. In any event, he didn't question Jym's caution.

Finally Jym asked *the* question: "What are we going to do with it?"

Kaylor had thought about this. "I believe it's a male of the species, and he may come in handy," he began. "This creature obviously was cargo aboard the ship. He could be a witness to what happened, verifying that pirates attacked the ship, and not us."

"Why did he attack *you*? We were not the ones who attacked the ship."

Kaylor let out a snort. "Well, only my ass was sticking out of the opening in the equipment bank. He probably thought I was one of the pirates."

"Then we'll have to convince him that we're not."

"That shouldn't be a problem, if this thing is intelligent enough to have a spoken language and if he doesn't go berserk when he wakes up. I don't know how civilized this thing is, but he acted like a wild animal when he attacked me."

"You should consider yourself lucky that you're not dead. Take a look at this." Jym led him over to a computer screen set in the wall above a small work desk. Punching a few keys, he pulled up an image that Kaylor recognized as a transparency scan.

"Before I bandaged the head wound, I took a scan of the skull to see how deep the puncture was. Look at this…" Jym pointed at the image, to a section indicating the thickness of the skull. "The bone structure is extremely dense and thick. The wound is shallow, but the trauma caused a slight swelling in the brain, right here. It will go down, and there shouldn't be any permanent damage."

"So? Good for him."

Jym glared at Kaylor, annoyed. Then he switched images. "Since the skull structure was so thick, I also did a full body scan, and here, look at the bones in the arm." On the screen was a cross section of what appeared to be an almost solid structure.

"That's a bone? It looks like some sort of metal rod."

"No, it's bone all right." Jym answered. "But just look how thick it is, easily twice as thick as yours or mine. No wonder your arm snapped like a twig when this thing hit you. And look at the muscle density. I'd hate to go up against this thing—ever—even in full body armor."

Kaylor studied the scan closer. He knew something about anatomy, since operating as an independent mule-driver on the fringe of civilization often meant having to fend for oneself for medical aid. He also knew from these scans that only the most primitive of creature had skeletal structures like this, an animal closer to the lower side of the evolutionary scale. Yes, Kaylor had been incredibly lucky. And now he had brought this thing aboard his ship…

"Put a monitor on him. We need to be very careful when he wakes up."

Jym and Kaylor were in the common area of the ship; Kaylor reclined on a couch, his injured arm resting on his chest, and in the other he held a 'stick, with its burning end quickly filling the room with a pungent cloud of dense, white smoke.

Jym was seated at the central table, gnawing on a piece of green filiean bark, which was the main staple of his people. He enjoyed its sweetness and texture, savoring each strand peeled from the bark as if it was a sexual experience. Even his eyes were glassy, but that may have had more to do with the smokestick in the room than anything else.

It had been over three hours since the meeting in the cargo hold, and during that time Kaylor had taken a shuttle pod over to the big ship and brought back a nav computer unit, a set of calibration tools and a few other smaller treasures he could easily stow in the pod. And now they were discussing their game plan for the upcoming salvage claim.

Between ripping bites of the bark, Jym was complaining. "I'm just saying: Reg 4 will hang us if we're caught."

Kaylor took another long drag off the 'stick and then blew the smoke into the air with flourish. "I know what Reg 4 says, Jym. If anyone asks, we'll just say the pirates must have taken the equipment before we got there. I just want to make sure we'll get something for all our effort, even if the salvage isn't granted."

Reg 4 was the law governing interstellar salvage procedures, and what they were referring to was the restriction that stated no items could be removed from a derelict until the salvage was registered and the proper chain of ownership investigated. Otherwise, it was simply piracy. By removing the computer core, along with the other items Kaylor had stored in the pod, they were technically just as guilty of a crime as the actual pirates themselves.

"I've checked the charts," Kaylor was saying. "We'll pass within a million kilometers of an asteroid belt once we get in the Nimorian system. I'll send the pod down to one of the bigger ones. They'll never find anything aboard the ship."

Jym knew Kaylor would be careful; he just liked to complain. All they had to do now is keep the creature in the cargo hold from seeing any of the booty, and they would be home free.

Almost on queue, Jym glanced over at the screen on the wall above Kaylor where the monitor in the cargo hold was displayed, and noticed the creature begin to stir on the workbench. He was waking up....

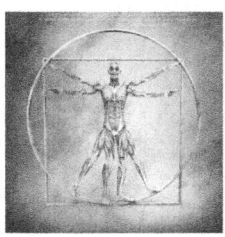

Chapter 4

The first thing he noticed was the smell. It was a sickly cross between rotting garbage and bad breath, and it almost made him gag. But as a dull consciousness returned, Adam fought with all his instincts to remember his survival training. First, he tried to remain still, learning all he could about his surroundings from the smell and sounds around him.

Yes, the smell was strange—like nothing he'd ever encountered—but the sounds he heard were non-threatening, just the soft whirl of a ventilation system and nothing else.

Then carefully, Adam opened his eyes, just a little, just enough to get a quick sense of where he was. He was in a large room with crates stacked against the far wall and three rows of light fixtures set into the ceiling. He was laying on some sort of hard surface, facing upwards. He didn't sense anyone else in the room.

Next, his training told him to assess his physical condition. He knew his head was injured, not only from the dull throbbing of his left temple, but the fact that he could now recall flying through the air and striking a hard metal wall with more force than he could imagine. Then he became aware of the burning sensation in his chest, and remembered a blue bolt of lightning flaring out at him—

The bastard shot me!

Trying to piece together the fragments of his dream/memory, Adam was at a loss to explain the sensation of flying he had experienced as he jumped at the thing in the blue tunic—and just kept going. He remembered all sense of balance leaving him and –it was all too confusing.

Anger swelled up inside him. Adam had no idea what was real or imagined, as the memories exploded in his head, filled with images of the Afghan mountains, then of a burning white light, and then of a soft bed with warm liquid flowing down his arm....

He awoke to find himself in a canister of some kind, and he pushed open the clear plastic dome and sat up. He was in a large, curving room with dozens of long canisters just like the one he was in, each with a clear, dome-shaped cover. From where he sat, Adam could see into six of the other canisters and each held another person; four men and two women, all naked, all asleep with needles and tubes in their arms.

He looked down at his arm. The needles had come out, and a warm, clear liquid was flowing from the tubes. He climbed out of the canister, his bare feet finding a cold metal surface; he stumbled, but caught himself against the side of the canister. His legs were weak, but he managed to regain his balance quickly.

And then came the most bizarre part of his dream/memory. To his left, he heard a high-pitched, screeching sound, and when he turned to investigate, he found himself staring down at an image he recognized from just about every science fiction movie he'd ever seen. It was about four feet tall, with a long gray head and large black eyes as big as pears. The thing was dressed in a one-piece gray jumpsuit—*and it was yelling at him!*

The tiny creature was upset, gesturing with its impossibly-thin arms, in an obvious fit of temper. Adam had seen enough. Grabbing a sheet from the canister, he turned on his heel and ran off in the opposite direction from the gray creature, wrapping the sheet around himself as he went. He was dizzy and confused, not knowing if this was a hallucination or reality. So he ran, past rows and rows of identical canisters, each containing a tranquil, sleeping person.

There was a doorway to his right, and he bolted through it into a wide, curving corridor. Turning left, he sprinted down the hallway until he saw a single door set in the wall to his right. Approaching it, he could not find a knob, so he placed his hand in a small depression about halfway down the door, and the panel slid silently into the wall on its own.

Adam slipped inside. It was a small utility room, with a single recessed light in the ceiling. Shelves lined three of the walls, all filled with boxes of various sizes. He closed the door and immediately the light went out.

He didn't panic. The darkness was his friend, giving him comfort from his nightmare. He crouched down and tried to calm his breathing in an effort to hear if anyone—or any-*thing*—was following him. But all was quiet.

He must have remained in the room for what seemed like twenty minutes or more, and then just as he was building up the courage to look outside, all hell broke loose.

He was in some kind of earthquake. The floor heaved up, and then dropped out from under him. He fell hard on his shoulder, as the whole room seemed to buck from left to right. Boxes from the shelves rained down upon him and he covered his head with his arms before crawling onto the lower shelf for cover.

And then it was over.

All was quiet again—for a moment.

Next, he heard and felt an explosion reverberate throughout the whole structure, followed quickly by the sounds of running in the corridor, along with electric popping sounds and high-pitched screams of agony.

Staying perfectly quiet, Adam dared not venture a look into the corridor. The popping sounds soon ended, but he could still hear movement outside in the hallway. He was in total darkness, yet mentally he tried to prepare himself for the moment the light would pop on meaning the door was opening....

But it never came. Instead, about ten minutes later, there came more sounds from the hallway. This time there were voices, and frantic ones at that. He didn't recognize the language, but after half a dozen missions in Afghanistan and Iraq, not recognizing a language wasn't all that unusual. Besides, what about the tiny gray creature....

People were calling out to others, and there was the sound of running on the metal floor, all in the direction to Adam's right. Then silence once again descended on the scene.

When all was quiet for another ten minutes or so, Adam slipped out of his hiding place in the shelving unit and felt his way in the darkness to the opposite wall where the door was set. Feeling the surface of the door, he found the recessed area again and the door slid open, light flooding in, temporarily blinding him. Cautiously, he stepped out into the corridor, listening intently for any signs of danger.

He knew that people had run down the corridor to his right, so he turned left. After about twenty meters, he came upon a bundle of sickeningly-burning flesh that had once been one of the gray creatures from before. He had seen some grisly things in war before, but he never got used to the acrid odor of burning flesh and hair. It was obvious a battle had taken place inside the building, and here he was, unarmed and naked except for a sheet wrapped around his waist.

Just then he heard a noise, as if a heavy metal box had hit the floor. He moved toward the sound, which seemed to come from the top of a wide stairway on his left. Climbing the stairs silently in his bare feet, Adam found himself in a narrow, circular room with what looked like a series of computer consoles to his right and to his left—it was the rear end of someone sticking out of an opening in a rack of equipment modules!

Approaching quietly, Adam wasn't about to let this—whatever it was—fry him like it had the little gray things....

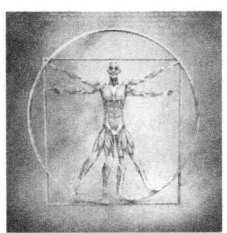

Chapter 5

Kaylor and Jym watched the monitor as the creature shook his head, then noticing the straps holding him down to the table, began jerking and twisting, doing his best to break free. Then frustrated, a sound came through the speakers, loud and primal, as the creature let out a scream: "Let me go, you motherfuckers!"

Moments later, Kaylor and Jym entered the cargo hold, Kaylor armed with this MK-17 bolt launcher. This time he made sure to set it at level-one. It would reduce the charge to only five bolts, but he was sure it could now stop the creature, should the need arise again.

The creature's piercing blue eyes flared as he watched the two of them enter the room, his mouth displaying double rows of long, white teeth. *Definitely a meat eater,* Kaylor concluded, which sent a shiver down his spine.

Approaching the bench, Kaylor rested his good hand on the butt of the launcher and tapped it gently with his fingers. The creature noticed the movement and seemed to acknowledge the fact that Kaylor had a weapon. *Not so dumb after all, are you?*

"Who—what are you?" The creature asked in a deep, strong voice. There didn't seem to be any fear in the question.

"I'm Kaylor, and this is Jym. And what is your name?"

The creature cocked his head slightly. "I don't understand. Are you speaking Farsi?"

This was strange. Kaylor and Jym exchanged a look, before Jym moved closer to the bench and reached out his hand toward the creature's head.

"Stay away from me, you stinking freak!"

Ignoring the protests, Jym pulled back the ear of the creature and felt the skin. Nothing—no trace at all. This thing truly was primitive.

Jym hurried out of the room, as Kaylor leaned against a crate and watched the creature, who stared back at him with a look of fierce defiance. *Go ahead and glare at me you animal,* Kaylor thought. *I'm not about to let you get the best of me. Not again.*

The thing was just standing there, staring at him. Adam had already accepted the fact that he wasn't dreaming; this was all too real. And even if it was a ruse, the makeup and special effects were way beyond anything the Taliban or Al Qaeda could do. Besides, why would they even bother going through all of this? They weren't known for their subtlety or sophistication.

So this was real, which meant this was a *real* alien standing in front of him.

The creature stood about his height, with pasty white skin that actually showed the pale purple traces of veins underneath. Its build was slight, yet proportional, and it didn't appear to be very muscular. But it was the face that was so—alien. The nose was extremely wide, with hardy a rise associated with it, and the eyes were very narrow and set wide apart. The mouth was small, with thin lips, and when it spoke, Adam noticed upper and lower rows of very small, slightly rounded teeth. On its head grew very little hair, grayish in color and mainly at the sides, wrapping around two very small, almost non-existent ears. And just below the ears dangled two, inch-long fingers of skin, for what purpose Adam was afraid to speculate.

Going lower, Adam saw two thin arms—one with what was clearly a cast on it—which ended with normal looking hands; four fingers and a thumb. Around the torso the creature wore a white wrap of some kind, tightly fitted over a light blue set of coveralls.

The overall affect was both alien and familiar at the same time. But whatever it was, it had him tied to a table, unable to move, and that made this alien-thing his enemy.

The smaller, hairy alien came rushing back into the room carrying a small box about the size of a ring case. It came up along the side of the table, opened the box and took something out. Adam struggled to move away as the creature reached toward his head, and then Adam felt a warm sensation on the skin behind his ear. The warmth quickly turned to a burning, stinging pain that quickly subsided. The small creature backed away.

"Can you hear me now?" The phrase caught Adam by surprise, not so much from its content, but from the fact that the movement of the creature's mouth did not match the words he heard.

Hesitantly, Adam responded. "Yeah, I can hear you. You speak English?"

"Your language is in the Library, that's all," the thing said. Again, the non-synchronized mouth and sounds reminded him of watching T.V. with the sound slightly out of synch. It was unnerving.

"What the hell am I doing here? And what ... what *are* you?"

The two creatures looked at each other, and Adam noticed a mutual reaction from both. The big one then stepped forward.

"Like I said, I am Kaylor and this is Jym." The voice came over as strong and confident, if slightly higher-pitched than Adam's. "Who are you?"

Alarms went off in Adam's mind, and again, his training took over. "Petty Officer 2nd Class Adam Cain, United States Navy. That's all I have to tell you."

The big one—Kaylor—gave a look of disgust. "That seems like a very long name. Do we call you Petty? Or Officer ... or what?"

"No, petty officer is my rank. Petty Officer 2nd Class. My name is Adam Cain."

"Hello Adam Cain."

"You can just call me Adam." This was getting ridiculous.

Kaylor's head bounced from left to right. "Very well, Adam. You're aboard my ship, the *FS-475*, and you are now safe."

Adam jerked against the straps holding him to the table. "If I'm safe, then why am I tied down here?" But not waiting for an answer, he went ahead and asked the most monumental question of his life: "Are you ... *aliens?*"

The two creatures exchanged another look, and then the small one spoke. "If you refer to someone who is not from where you come from, and is different from you, then I submit it is *you* who is the alien here, not us." The tone, even for an alien, was sarcastic and condescending.

Kaylor placed a hand on Jym's arm. "To you, yes, we would be aliens. But the term doesn't have much meaning to us. There are so many other worlds and races that no one is truly *alien*. Where are *you* from?"

"I'm not tellin' you shit! I saw what you did to those other ... things."

"I did not do that. I came aboard later——"

"He saved your life!" Jym blurted out.

If Adam had not already seen the tiny gray beings he was sure he would have been in complete amazement with the fact that here he was talking with two very real-life "aliens." But the shock had passed, replaced now with a seething anger. He was being held prisoner, and that was all that mattered now.

He tried to calm down, and he closing his eyes for a moment while taking in a couple of deep breaths. He would have liked to have spent more time trying to reason with the aliens to release him, but that wasn't going to be possible, not now. When he regained his composure, Adam had only one thing on his mind.

"Listen," he started slowly, "if you don't let me loose pretty soon, and show me where the closest bathroom is, we're going to have a real mess around here."

"Bath, room?" Again, the two aliens looked at each other.

"Yeah, bathroom, restroom, head, latrine, whatever you call it here. I have to relieve myself, and I mean right now!"

The two aliens appeared to panic. Adam got the distinct impression that they hadn't planned on this. Finally Kaylor spoke. "We can't risk untying you. You nearly killed me before. Is there anything else we can do?"

"Like what, give me a bedpan? No, you're going to have to let me loose, and quickly."

Making a decision, Kaylor stepped away from the table and drew his weapon. "This is set for a level-one max bolt. This time it *will* kill you. Do not attempt to attack either one of us." His head shook back and forth again, this time in the direction of Jym, who stepped forward and began to loosen the straps.

Soon Adam was free, and he jumped off the table. He was light headed, but could still function reasonably well. "Follow Jym," Kaylor commanded. "I'll be behind you at a safe distance."

Obeying, Adam was led out of the warehouse and into a narrow, dimly-lit hallway. About ten meters down, Jym slid open a door and Adam stepped into what was a restroom of strange familiarity. There was a bank of sinks and even some dirty mirrors on the wall above them. Against another wall were two seats with holes placed in them. *What do you know, the aliens use toilets!*

Adam quickly slipped past Jym and plopped down on the nearest seat, separating the filthy sheet he still wore as he did so.

Then looking at the two aliens, he said, "Do you mind; how about a little privacy?"

"While relieving yourself? Why?" Kaylor asked.

"It's just how we do it. Please."

Reluctantly, the two aliens backed out of the room and slid the door shut. Adam should have been thinking about looking for a way out, but first things first—he really had to go.

Once he was done, he looked around for some toilet paper and a flush handle, but found none. All he saw was a blue button on the wall to his right. He pushed it, and immediately felt a warm sensation on his butt, and then a small puff of smoke wafted up to be immediately sucked into a vent at the toilet bowl lining.

And that was that. He felt clean and there was no residue in the bowl. *Pretty neat*, he thought. Advanced alien shitter technology....

Now it was time to get down to business. Standing up, Adam began to survey the room for another door or a window, any avenue of escape. Instead his gaze fell upon an image in one of the dirty mirrors. It was of a gaunt man with a short, straggly beard and a crop of longish, oily blond hair. *Was it him?*

He moved closer. What had happened? It was indeed and image of him in the mirror, but now his formerly clean shaven face easily displayed a two- or three-week growth of beard, while there was two to three inches of hair on his normally crew-cut head. Being a sailor—and especially with his rating—he had kept the hair on his head down to a bare minimum. Now look at him. He must have been unconscious for a lot longer than he thought.

But the scariest part of it all—it seemed like only a few hours had passed since he was on patrol in the Kush, with Zack and Peanut and the rest of the guys from his Team. And he'd lost weight, too—a lot of it in fact. So he must have been under for a good two to three weeks, probably more.

Then as he stood staring at the stranger in the mirror, another thought came crashing down upon him: *Maria and Cassie!*

He broke out into a cold sweat and began to tremble violently. If he had been unconscious for what could be weeks, either in the warehouse room or in that canister, then what was happening with his wife and two-year-old daughter? If he had been captured—wait, abducted—then he would have been reported as missing in action. His knees grew weak and he nearly collapsed, steadying himself on the sink. *What were they going through?* he thought. *My God, they must think I'm dead!*

Just then, the door to the restroom slid open and the tall alien with the gun entered. "That's long enough. Let's get back—"

Adam suddenly spun around facing the alien, his eyes wide, his bottom lip trembling. "My family—they think I'm dead!"

Kaylor gripped the weapon tighter, preparing for something that never came.

Instead, Adam dropped to his knees and held his head in his hands. Then looking up at Kaylor through tear-filled eyes, he said, "You've got to get me back home. They can't go on believing I was killed, or even worse, captured by those savages."

Kaylor began to say something, but then stopped. Slowly, he lowered his weapon. Jym moved in quickly next to him. "What are you doing?"

"Let us all go down to the common room. We have much to discuss."

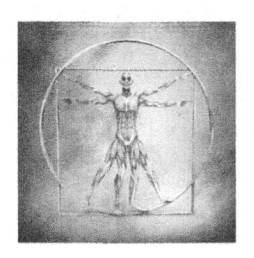

Chapter 6

A few minutes later, Adam had regained his composure and was seated at the table in the center of the common room area, a room that resembled a combination dining hall and lounge area. He felt as if he was losing his mind, as the events of the past few hours all came crashing down upon him. A strange numbness filled his body and he appeared to be just going through the motions as he was lead down a series of ladders and then into the room where he now found himself. Even looking at the strangeness of the other two occupants of the room didn't seem to faze him.

"Would you like something to drink?" the tall alien asked.

Adam simply nodded, but instead of bringing him something in a glass, the creature—Kaylor was his name—laid a small box on the table in front of him. Adam just looked up at him.

After a moment, Kaylor reacted. "You truly are primitive," he said with disgust. "It's a sampling box. It is used to test your blood to see what food and drink you can tolerate. Do you not have anything like this where you come from?"

"Nah, we just eat whatever don't make us sick," came Adam's feeble reply. Kaylor told him to stick his finger in the box. There was a slight prick of pain and then Kaylor took the box away. He placed it in a slot above a table jutting from the wall and almost instantly a panel slid open, and inside was a glass of brownish liquid. Kaylor brought the glass over to the table and sat down opposite Adam. The smaller one—Jym was his name—was seated on a couch, about as far away from Adam as he could get.

Still in a daze, Adam took the glass and sampled some of its contents. Not bad, kind of like Coke, even with some carbonation. It was then that he noticed how dry his throat was, as the liquid burned a path down to his stomach and then it hit there, setting off an explosion of gurgles and rumbling like he'd never experienced before.

"How long was I out for?" he asked finally, once his stomach had settled down.

"Not more than a couple of hours."

"How about in that canister, where the other people were?"

"That I do not know. Like I said, we came upon that ship later on, after the pirates had already attacked it."

Pirates? Ships? What was this, a Disney ride? But wait—

"You're not talking about ships at sea, are you? We're in space?"

Adam was beginning to recognize the look of confusion on the faces of the aliens, and here it was again. "Of course we're in space."

"And this is *another* spaceship? A different one than I was on before?"

"Correct. This is my ship. Mine and Jym's."

This was all fascinating, but Adam was beginning not to care about any of this. Instead, he cut to the chase. "I have to get back home. Can you take me there?"

"Where are you from?"

"Cali—I mean I'm from Earth."

Jym appeared to burst into laughter, or what Adam took as alien laughter. "You're from the planet 'Dirt?' That is not a very creative name for a planet."

Adam had decided that he really didn't like this particular creature very much.

"No, *Earth* not dirt."

Kaylor stepped into the conversation: "The translation we're hearing has it as dirt, soil, ground—things like that. But we can amend the translator to give your planet the designation of Earth."

"Thank you. But how can I understand what you're saying now?"

"It's the translator bug—device—Jym placed behind your ear. Everyone has one, except you. Your planet appears to be very primitive."

Even through his stupor, Adam felt the hairs on the back of his neck rise up from the backhanded insult. But he said nothing. Instead, he watched as Jym crossed the room and sat down at a small desk. He punched a few keys on an in-laid keyboard and began to read. Adam could see the writing on the screen, but he couldn't read any of it. It was all Greek to him.

"Earth, the home planet of the Human race," he began, "including the Afghanis, Americans, Armenians ... whoa! There's a whole list of races that come from your planet."

"Those aren't races. They're countries, or people from those countries."

"You mean your planet is divided into all these different groups? But you're all of the same species, correct?" Jym's voice was again laced with a condescending tone.

"Yeah, that's right." Adam took the last gulp of his drink. "Can you take me there or not?"

Jym turned back to the screen. After a moment of scanning the readout, he turned back toward Adam and said, "Not feasible. Earth is rumored to be located in the Far Arm. Actual location, unknown."

The words hit Adam like a punch in the face. "What does that mean, the Far Arm? Don't you guys have charts or maps you can follow? And how can it be unknown if you know my language?" He could feel the panic growing in his chest. "Hey, I didn't sign up for this! I've got to get back home."

Kaylor took a deep breath. "Languages are assimilated into the Library without reference or source. This simply means that your planet has been visited before—as your presence here also testifies. But being in the Far Arm, which is a wilderness to us, means that the location of your world has never been accurately ascertained. And if this is the case, then there is nothing we can do to get you back—"

"And even if we knew where it was known, it would cost a fortune to take you there." Jym interrupted.

"This is bullshit!" Adam yelled.

That look of confusion came over Kaylor's face once again. "I do not understand the connotation between some kind of animal excrement and your situation," he said.

"Bullshit. BULLSHIT! It means this is unbelievable. Like I said, I didn't ask to be here, and I *demand* that you take me back."

Kaylor stood up, and began to draw his weapon, yet before his hand could reach the grip, Adam reached out and grabbed his wrist. Kaylor winched in pain.

"Don't even think about it." Adam spat out between gritted teeth. "I don't want to hurt you guys; I actually believe this isn't your fault. But I'm pretty pissed off right about now and I'm in a terrible mood."

Kaylor fell back in the chair and placed his hands on the table in front of him. Jym sat stunned at the little desk, his mouth agape.

"You don't seem to understand me, pal," said Adam, leaning in closer and staring straight into Kaylor's eyes. "I have a wife and a kid back home, and they're probably going through Hell right now, thinking that I'm dead, and that's just something I can't live with. Someone, somewhere is going to take me back to …" he found it so hard to say, "… back to Earth."

Kaylor began to bob his head back and forth again, a movement Adam now recognized as a nod of agreement. "We will do everything we can to help you, Adam Cain. But you must realize, we do not know where your planet is located, and our ship is not capable of finding it. The Far Arm is a mostly unexplored region of space for us."

"What about that other ship, the one you said I was on? They should know where Earth is. After all, that's where they kidnapped me from!"

"All the occupants of the other ship are dead."

"What about any records, logs, computer disks, or anything like that?"

Kaylor tensed. "The computer core was stolen by the pirates. I'm afraid there are no other records."

"Who are these god-damn pirates?" Adam slammed his fist down hard on the table, denting it, and sending a loud report throughout the room.

"We don't know who they are. They are a menace here in The Void, and throughout The Fringe. No one knows who they are or where they come from."

"Bullshit! Somebody knows."

Kaylor hesitated, and then said, "No…no bullshit. All I can promise you is that when we get to Nimor, we will turn you over to the Ministry, and maybe they can help you."

Adam leaned back in the chair, exhausted, pissed off and confused. He rubbed his eyes and just shook his head. What should have been the greatest adventure for all of mankind was rapidly turning into a freaking nightmare. If no one knew where he came from—and he could never return home—then he might as well be dead. After all, in the eyes of the military, as well as those of his wife and young daughter, he already was.

As he sat there with his eyes closed, in a room with two very smelly aliens, Adam once again fought to maintain control. He was supposed to know how to handle difficult situations like these, but the rollercoaster of emotions he was experiencing wouldn't stop. Never in the training manuals did they cover how to cope with being abducted by aliens.

Suddenly he felt a wave of hopelessness sweep over him. Maybe he should let Kaylor pull out his weapon blow his brains out. It really didn't matter anymore. At least then all the pain and confusion would go away. It would end his nightmare, as well as all the memories.

But Kaylor did not draw his weapon. Instead he motioned for Jym to follow him, and they left Adam alone in the common room.

Once back in the pilothouse, Jym spoke first. "That was close. We can never let him know about the computer core."

"Agreed, but I believe we could use his testimony regarding the pirates and the salvage. But we have to be careful with him."

Jym's ears were flicking wildly. "Agreed, that thing is dangerous," he said, as he paced the room. "We need to get rid of him as soon as possible. And can you believe that he wants us to shuttle him back to some unknown planet in the Far Arm! That's crazy. Does he think we're made of credits? I don't know how it is on his world, but everything has a price in the *real* galaxy."

Kaylor let him vent; it was just his way.

"Put him in number three and make him comfortable. We'll be at Nimor in about twenty hours. After that, he will be someone else's problem."

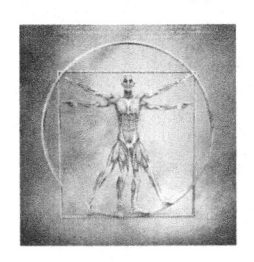

Chapter 7

In a daze, Adam allowed himself to be led to a room with a small bed and a desk set into a wall. The chair for the desk was affixed to the floor and on the desk sat small a monitor screen. Adam chose to sit on the end of the bed rather than at the desk. Jym handed him a blue tunic and a pair of slip-on shoes, similar to what Kaylor wore.

"I'll bring you some food in a while," Jym said. "Until then, please attempt to rest." He then pointed out a small control panel near the door. "If you need more or less gravity to make yourself comfortable, you can do it from here."

This comment snapped Adam out of his stupor. "You can adjust *gravity?*"

"Of course." Jym had to fight back the urge to add another comment about Adam's primitive pedigree, but instead he simply said, "There are five individual wells which control the ship's internal gravity. You appear to come from a heavy-gravity world, so you may want to adjust it up some. We'll be on Nimor in about twenty hours." The tiny alien then abruptly turned and left room.

Adam looked around his surroundings; again familiar, yet strange. His mind knew he was so far away from anything native to him that it was unimaginable, and yet here he was, alive, in relatively good condition and in the company of two very real aliens who did not appear to be a threat to him. Yet all of this didn't help his overall situation, or his mood.

He stood up and went over to the control panel by the door. He touched it, and the panel lit up. There was a digital scale with a cursor (again familiar), and when he moved the cursor up, he immediately felt as if a weight was pressing down on his body. The sensation quickly passed, so he moved the cursor up a little more, with the same effect. One more move, and he felt as if his weight was maybe a little heavier than what he was used to. Since there was nothing to compare it to, he went simply by feel.

It suddenly occurred to him that maintaining his strength advantage in these alien surroundings would be very important. He knew that he was much stronger than these two aliens, and that if he didn't keep that advantage, he could be in serious trouble. Not being familiar with their technology or customs, it may be the only thing that he had going for him.

So he cranked the cursor up even more, and felt the immediate pressure on his body. Having trained more than just about any other Human being for his job in the Navy, Adam knew the added weight would be like carrying a backpack around with him, keeping him as strong as possible, and ready for just able any contingency.

He returned to the bed and laid down, resting his head on the hard pillow he propped against the bulkhead wall. The first thing he had to do was get his mind around his situation. As much as the physical, his mental condition would also play a major role in determining if he survived or not.

He chuckled. Just moments before he didn't give a damn if he lived or died. Now he was thinking about how to survive. The Human spirit sure was resilient....

As he lay there, Adam began to take inventory of his predicament.

He was/had been a 26-year-old E-5 in the US Navy, a member of the elite DEVGRU group, which most of the Team members still referred to as SEAL Team Six. In his SMU, or Special Mission Unit, he was classified as a sniper and weapons expert, even though nearly everyone in his unit carried the same designation. He had been on his fourth excursion in-country, this time on a recon of the rugged mountain area between Afghanistan and Pakistan known as the Hindu Kush. They had been following a lead on a Taliban commander who had taken credit for a recent bombing of the US Embassy in Kabul—when his whole world was suddenly jerked out from under him.

His future in the Navy was looking bright. He had just completed his advanced sniper instructor training, and had also taken the First Class exam the month before. He felt confident that he would make E-6, since SEALs were a pretty dedicated group of sailors, and he was no exception to that rule. If he made E-6, then there was a good chance he could come back to Dam Neck as an instructor.

Seven months ago, just after he'd returned from his third mission to Afghanistan, he and Maria had bought their first home, located in a quiet cul-de-sac off Lynnhaven Parkway in Virginia Beach, Virginia. It was a small three bedroom, two bath brick home, with a one-car attached garage. More than anything else, Adam had bought the home for the garage, where he kept his mint-condition 2006 Mustang GT under a blue canvas tarp.

His daughter Cassie was two at the time, and Adam felt guilty having to leave Maria on her own every time he was sent out, what with the new house and the terrible-two's all at once. But if he made First Class, he could apply as an instructor and that would guarantee him at least three years in Hampton Roads. And with the war winding down, it could possibly be even longer.

Adam's dad had been career Navy, too, and was extremely proud of his only son. David Cain lived in Northern California—Monterey to be precise—and he and his son exchanged emails nearly every day, at least when Adam wasn't off on a mission somewhere or in advanced training.

The thought of his father sent a spasm of pain through Adam's heart. By now, his dad would have also accepted the fact that his son was dead, more than likely taken captive and tortured to death by the Taliban. Since Adam knew his body would never be recovered, and no publicity extracted from his capture, that would be the only assumption most people could make. After all, his Teammates would never have left his body on the battlefield—if there had been a body to recover.

In addition to his immediate family, Adam enjoyed a large circle of friends and other more-distant relatives, who by now would all be mourning his death. Most of them knew what he did for a living, and in reality, your odds of being violently killed were much higher living in Chicago these days, than spending time in a combat zone. However, it was always a possibility, even though most of his people chose not to dwell on it.

Damn! His future was—or had been—pretty set. Adam had always been a man of ambition and purpose, but his goals had never been to travel into space and meet aliens, at least outside of his childhood fantasies. Now his entire life was turned inside out. All his friends and loved ones were suffering from his supposed death, and here he was, very much alive, and yet unable to prove it to anyone.

Lying on the bed aboard the alien spacecraft, assessing his situation, it was obvious to him that he could easily overpower the two aliens and commandeer their spaceship. But then what? He didn't know how to fly it, and more importantly, he didn't have any idea where to go if he did. Space, after all, was a pretty big place. So that course of action was out of the question.

Also, the alien Kaylor didn't seem too confident that the creatures on the planet they were heading for could really help him. His statement to that affect sounded more like a way of pacifying Adam's anger, rather than any real possibility.

Adam felt the blood drain from his head, as he struggled against the onset of yet another anxiety attack. He had been trained to overcome and survive the most harrowing of situations—but this was ridiculous! How was one supposed to prepare for something like this?

Getting back to Earth was now his only priority, but this was a lot different than trying to make your way back to friendly forces after having been separated from his Teammates during a mission. He was light years away from his home, his family thought he was dead ... and—well damn, his prospects weren't looking very good right about now!

He could just give up, and hasten the inevitable. Or ... he could learn to survive in this alien environment and bide his time until a solution could be found.

Adam closed his eyes and took several deep breaths. When he opened his eyes again, he felt a wave of relief flow over him.

In reality, it doesn't really matter what I do. I can either live or die; after all, what do I have to live for? Everyone I know thinks I'm dead already, and I'm in a universe where I'm the alien! The only thing that matters now is getting home, and if I can't do that, then who cares what happens to me? I'm like the walking dead....

Adam suddenly realized that not caring—*really not caring*—about what happens to you can be a very liberating experience. And unfortunately for those around him, if he didn't care what happens to himself, he definitely didn't care what happens to anyone—or any*thing*—else he encountered along the way.

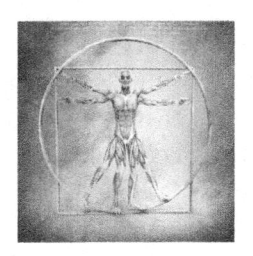

Chapter 8

Riyad entered the communication room where an underling was preparing the link. He sat down before the large monitor and nodded to the tech. An image appeared on the screen; it was the interior command room of Captain Angar's ship. Angar was facing him, but talking with someone off screen. As soon as he noticed the link had been established, he straightened up and gave his full attention to Riyad.

"General Riyad, sir, we have a solid link."

Riyad loved the title of *'General.'* Out of all the possibilities available to him, he had chosen this one for himself, and it sent a thrill drown his spine nearly every time he heard it. Yes, he knew he commanded a fleet of pirate *ships*, not land forces, but he was the only one who seemed to notice the inconsistency. However, looking at his subordinate on the screen, the thrill quickly passed, and he sent a steely stare at his senior captain.

"So what happened? I understand you had the ship completely under your control but then you gave it up."

Angar shifted nervously in his chair at the directness of the question, but then quickly regained his composure. "In my defense, *I* was the last one to bolt out. There was nothing I could do by myself, not against a fleet of Rigorian warships."

"And yet it ended up not being a *fleet* at all."

"That is correct, my General. It was a deception. But we had no way of knowing that at the time."

Riyad took a deep breath. "But Captain, you know, as well as I, that the Rigorians are not that aggressive against us. Also, we have never encountered them that far out in The Void."

"Again correct, my General. But when Jiden and Meldeon left, I had no choice but to follow."

"The two of them will be dealt with." Riyad stated acidly. "So where is the ship now?"

Angar glanced to his right, and then turned back to Riyad. "They are just now entering the Nimorian system. They should be making planet-fall in about six hours. We could attempt to catch up to them, but we will not be successful."

"Please tell me you were at least able to secure some treasure before you gave up the ship?"

Again, Angar shifted in his seat. "Unfortunately, no. There wasn't time, and the only cargo we could readily see appeared to be a room full of primes placed in stasis."

Even through his anger, this news piqued Riyad's curiosity. "Was this a slave ship?"

"Hard to tell, General. The primes were all in good condition and contained in very sophisticated hiberpods. There were around seventy to eighty of them in the room." Angar hesitated before continuing. "And they had all been recently killed by the ship's crew."

Riyad was taken aback by the last comment. "Killed, all of them? Why?"

"Impossible to tell. But it appeared they had been killed at about the same time we were assaulting the ship."

"What species were they?"

Angar seemed to grow even more nervous than he already was. Riyad noticed the body language. "What is it, Captain? What's the problem?"

"Well, my General," Angar began hesitantly, "they appear to be of the same race as *you*."

Riyad was sure Angar saw the look of total shock sweep over his face, and even though his mind was exploding with a thousand questions, he knew it was important to maintain his composure in front of his underlings.

"Can you confirm this information, Captain?" he managed to say, hoping that the timbre of his voice didn't give away his excitement.

"I saw them with my own eyes. I have no doubt. You are the only other one of your species I have ever seen, until today."

Riyad remained silent for a long moment, digesting the information. He had always suspected that this day would come. *Now this changes everything.*

"Captain Angar, I have new instructions for you," Riyad began evenly. "By my orders, you will have Captains Meldeon and Jiden return to K'ly. Then you will proceed to Nimor, and secure that ship's computer core and bring it to me immediately."

Angar looked stunned. "But General, the ship will be locked down until the salvage is settled."

"Do you think I care about that? We're *pirates*, after all; we don't go by the rules, Captain. Contact our allies in the Ministry. I want to know everything about that ship and where it came from. And Captain Angar," Riyad leaned in closer to the screen, "no one else is to get that computer core except us—no one. Don't screw this up again." And then he cut the link.

Riyad rushed out of the comm room and proceeded quickly to the forward section of his ship. As he neared his quarters, he felt the welcoming increase in gravity, a consequence that kept most of his crew out of his private sanctuary.

He entered his quarters and shut the door. Too excited to sit, Riyad began to pace the room, nervously.

Humans—and lots of them!

He had not seen another Human, for how long now? Six years, maybe longer? And here was a ship carrying dozens of his kin. Granted, Riyad had been more than a little surprised to hear that they had all been killed, but once he thought about it, it made perfect sense.

The aliens must know of our abilities.

This could also be the reason they were transporting the Humans in stasis. After all, look what Riyad had done with the Fringe Pirates—and he was just one Human. Imagine how hard it would have been to transport dozens of conscious Humans aboard one ship. Yes, these aliens definitely knew the capabilities of the Human race, and they had taken the only sensible course of action.

But the question had to be asked: What were they doing with that many Humans aboard their ship in the first place? And where were they taking them?

Mentally, Riyad shrugged off the questions. He was only obliquely interested in the answer, just as a curiosity. What he really wanted to know was how did they know the location of Earth in the first place?

Within the computer core of that ship was the Holy Grail of his existence for the past six years—*the coordinates to his homeworld!*

And quite possibly, the realization of a dream he had been cultivating for a very long time....

Riyad Tarazi had challenged the ship's captain for his position after only having been a crewmember for three months, but that been time enough for him to learn the operation of the ship, as well as the pirate hierarchy aboard.

The captain was a Fil-nipon—not even a native of The Fringe—but he was tough and strong, and had been part of the pirate community for almost twenty years. It had been a duel, and by this time, Riyad had no doubt as to the outcome. The captain's weapon had not even cleared its holster by the time Riyad had placed a level-one bolt through the creature's chest.

According to pirate law, Riyad Tarazi was now the Captain.

Nine months later, it was Riyad's time to challenge the supreme pirate leader for his position within the ragtag structure of the organization. Those nine months had given him time to study how the pirates operated, and how their operations could be greatly improved, under the right leadership, of course. At that time, the Fringe Pirates were just a loose-knit group of privateers, with no real purpose, other than their own individual gain. They did not operate as a unit, as force greater than that of any singular planetary military force this side of the Juireans. Riyad figured they would do much better under his leadership, and only the senior captain stood in his way.

The pirate leader was a Rigorian named Kymore, and he had heard of Riyad's prowess with a bolt weapon. So when he accepted the challenge he did so with one condition—it was to be a physical contest, and not one with weapons. Riyad had accepted his terms without a second thought.

Rigorians were the toughest, strongest and meanest natives of the Fringe. Giant lizard-like creatures, they grew scales for skin, and carried double rows of razor-sharp teeth lining a protruding, foot-long snout. In all the history of the Fringe, no one other than another Rigorian had ever bested a Rigorian in hand-to-hand combat. As the day of the contest neared, the Rigorian was feeling very confident about his chances.

Yet once again, Riyad had studied his opponent before making the challenge, so the outcome was never in doubt.

On the day of the challenge, a crowd of several hundred pirates all gathered in a field near the K'ly city of Calaa. A stage had been built where they would fight. It was all a festive and jubilant occasion.

Kymore began the event by loudly proclaiming his superiority with a series of grunts and howls while prancing around the stage, showing off his size and quickness. Riyad just stood off to the side and let the lizard do his thing.

And then the fight began. Riyad easily slipped around each of the alien's initial thrusts, and then after a minute or so of dancing around the stage, placed a swift kick to the Rigorian's side. The kick knocked most of the air out of Kymore's lungs, bringing a look of startled confusion to his yellow eyes. Riyad then slipped quickly behind the pirate and placed a solid blow to the back of the lizard's head. Kymore fell forward onto the stage, but quickly rolled over and regained his feet.

There was an even greater look of concern now on the Rigorian's face, and for the next few seconds, Riyad pummeled the pirate leader with rights and lefts, causing prodigious amounts of blood to flow from the creature's mouth. And then, simply as a display of his superior strength, Riyad hoisted the seven-foot tall alien above his head and threw him into the front row of stunned pirates, all in perfect Hulk Hogan fashion.

A dozen pirates fell into a heap of alien flesh, but they soon recovered, and forced the panicked Rigorian back onto the stage.

During his time with the pirates, Riyad had heard where other challenges for the pirate leadership had ended simply with the demotion of the current leader, and not his death. This didn't make sense to Riyad. After assuming his new position, he did not want any lingering loyalties for his predecessor or grumblings for his return.

So for the finale, Riyad grasped the massive jaws of the lizard and pulled them open wide. He continued to spread them apart, until he felt the bottom jaw of the Rigorian break. The creature let out a piercing, blood-curding scream, and fell to his knees, his bottom jaw dangled limply down from his head. The crowd was stunned into silence.

Riyad then moved ceremoniously behind Kymore, took a moment to survey the silent crowd, and then drove his right fist all the way down into the lizard's skull, killing him instantly—while also assuring there would no challenges to Riyad's leadership, at least for a long while.

That should get their attention, he thought, as he looked out as the silent mass of pirates before him. Pirates were like a pack of wolves, subservient to the alpha male. And at that moment, the alpha male of The Fringe Pirates was the Human Riyad Tarazi.

He was now the Pirate *General.*

As Riyad paced his quarters, recalling his ascension to the leadership of The Fringe Pirates, he nodded his approval. Yes, the aliens aboard that ship had been wise to assassinate the Humans, rather than have them fall into the hands of the pirates. After all, they couldn't afford to have dozens of crazed Humans out wandering the galaxy, causing all kinds of havoc, now could they?

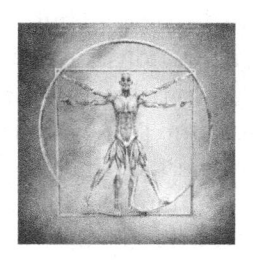

Chapter 9

Over the 24-hour transit to Nimor, Adam and the two aliens had very little contact. Jym had dropped off some bland tasting food—*yes, it tasted like chicken*—and then left without saying a word.

Adam was able to get some good rest, and he even found a shower in the ship's only restroom. He dressed in the blue tunic and waited in his room for the next hammer to fall. He didn't know what it would be, but he was about to make landfall on an alien world where Kaylor and Jym would turn him over to other group of aliens—and from there, who knew? Even though he'd only been aboard their ship for a few hours, he did feel a strange familiarity with them and his surroundings. What this new alien world held in store for him would be just one more shock to his already frazzled system.

Kaylor allowed Adam to join them in the pilothouse as he released the alien spaceship into an orbit above Nimor. Another alien—short, hairy and husky—came aboard with an entourage of bureaucrats and Kaylor led them through a quick inspection of his ship. Apparently satisfied, the burly alien had Kaylor sign some paperwork and then he left, indicating that his crew was now going aboard the big disk-shaped ship to start the salvage inventory. The completed survey would be transmitted to the Ministry in about three hours, they were told.

Kaylor opened the exterior shield to the pilothouse viewport and Adam gazed out at a vast and brilliant alien world. It looked very similar to Earth, with shimmering blue seas and ruddy brown land masses, all with patchy white clouds casting dark shadows on the surface below. This world didn't appear to have as much landmass as Earth, just a modest-sized blob to the north and a large island to the south. He didn't know if there was more land on the other side, because they didn't seem to be moving around the planet while in orbit—they call it geo-synchronous, he believed.

Jym asked Adam to strap himself into a seat next to him and Kaylor began the decent to the planet's surface.

Adam was struck by the fact that he felt no sensation of falling, or any movement at all as a matter of fact. He simply watched as the features on the ground grew larger until he could make out the criscrossed pattern of a city below. As they got closer, the ship slid over toward a large open area dotted with various craft of different shapes and sizes. As they descended, Adam was amazed at how large the area was, and how massive some of the ships actually were close up.

His view was suddenly obscured by dense clouds of dust that appeared to streaming upward past the viewport. And then he felt a slight bump.

"Prepare yourself, I'm dissolving the well." Kaylor announced to the room. Instantly, Adam felt light-headed, and he felt a good portion of his bodyweight melt away.

Jym noticed Adam's reaction. "This planet is about .75 of standard. I'm guessing that would make it a little more than half the gravity of your world. You should get along fine here, if you don't stay too long."

"We'll see," was all he could muster.

The three of them left the pilothouse and Kaylor told Adam that Jym would be staying on the ship while the two of them went into the Nimorian city of Gildemont to the Ministry Compound to register the salvage. Adam was surprised to see Kaylor was wearing his weapon around his waist.

"So what's this place like?" he asked.

"It's not the roughest place in the Fringe, but close. They've only been members of the Expansion for about twenty years, so they still have a lot of tribal factions who go by their own rules. The Ministry is more of a suggestion here rather than any real authority. They have a compound not too far into the city. All I want to do is get the salvage officially registered, and then we can leave. It will take a couple of months before any resolution is decided."

"What does that mean?"

"Simply bringing in a derelict ship doesn't convey ownership rights. The ship will have to be matched against any missing vessel reports, and then if the rightful owners come forward, we'll get a salvage reward of ten-percent of the ship's value. If the owner's cannot pay, or no one comes forward to claim ownership, then we will be awarded full ownership. All that takes time, but once we file the salvage, our rights are protected."

"That makes sense." Adam said. "So this is a pretty big deal for you?"

"It could definitely be worth the effort, eventually."

They were standing before a door set in an outer wall of the cargo hold and when Kaylor pushed a button on a small control panel the door slid open. Warm, dry air rushed in, smelling sweet and fresh. Adam hadn't realized just how stale the air in the ship had been. This was refreshing. They stepped down a metal ramp that projected from the ship, and soon Adam Cain set foot on an alien world.

"That's one small step for man…" he began softly.

"What did you say?"

"Oh nothing—nothing that's important anymore."

It was a pretty good hike through the forest of alien spaceships parked in what Kaylor told him was a modest-sized, yet rundown spaceport, but Adam found it all fascinating. There was also a menagerie of exotic creatures all around; tall ones, short ones, disgusting looking things and even some that were kind of pretty. They all went about their business not giving Adam or Kaylor a second glance.

They eventually passed through a gate with a bored looking blob of a creature manning a rundown metal booth who seemed not to even notice their passing.

The sun was warm on his skin and it helped to loosen the tense muscles in his neck, muscles that had been knotted up a lot more than he realized. The humidity was low, and it actually felt like his home growing up in Southern California. A slight breeze stirred brown dust, adding a musty smell to the landscape as they proceeded down the side of a dirt road toward the city proper. Adam found it all incongruous; starships and dirt roads. High tech combined with low tech.

Adam was also very aware of the light gravity of this world. On Earth he weighed in at around 190 pounds, so here he was just over a hundred.

So can I jump twice as high, or run twice as fast? He certainly felt as if he could.

So he thought he'd experiment. He fell back slightly behind Kaylor as they walked, and then crouching down he sprung upwards with all the effort his leg muscles could manage. Up he went, easily soaring as high as Kaylor was tall, which was close to Adam's height of six-foot-one. Kaylor couldn't help but notice the sudden movement, and he jumped back, placing his hand on the grip of his weapon.

"What did you do that for?" Kaylor yelled, a look of concern plastered on his alien face.

"I just wanted to see if I could."

"A word of advice: Don't go showing off around here. Most of the inhabitants are barely out of the trees, and they will take most actions as a challenge."

Adam just smiled back at him. Yes, it might be better to keep any special abilities he may have close to the vest for now. First he had to size up the locals. He had done this on numerous occasions before during his Navy career. *Just be cool until you learn the local customs.*

They were soon in the town, walking on a wooden sidewalk past storefronts with glass windows. It was so Old West that Adam had trouble remembering he was on an alien planet. However, all it took was for a hairy, rodent-looking creature to walk out of a doorway on its two hind legs to shock him back into reality.

Adam was also disappointed to see numerous wheeled vehicles moving up and down the road. No hovercraft or anti-gravity machines. These were very similar to small SUV's, and they even seemed to be obeying traffic rules rather than running around all helter-skelter.

Regarding the Ministry, Kaylor wasn't kidding about it being a 'Compound.' The Ministry Complex, the official government headquarters for this entire planet, was a sprawling arrangement of buildings all sequestered behind a massive four-meter-tall stone wall, with one large opening guarded by four gruff-looking creatures a little shorter than Adam. Each of the alien guards were covered with a black coat of hair or fur and wearing leather-like vests and pants, and were of the same species as those who had come aboard Kaylor's ship earlier. They carried long-barrel weapons along with sidearms like the one Kaylor wore.

Kaylor informed one of the guards that he was there to register a salvage and was directed to Building Five without so much as a second glance by the other guards. So far, everything Adam had seen on the surface of Nimor was of this same casual, nonchalant—even uncaring—manner. No one seemed that concerned with security or protocol.

Building Five was built of red brick and stood four stories tall. The two of them entered through double glass doors and were directed to the second floor, Room 12. Inside the room was another black-haired creature—obviously the natives to this world—who directed them to both takes seats in front of the official's.

"I'm Fredic Dess," the hairy creature stated in a deeper-than-expected voice. Adam still wasn't accustomed to the unsynchronized movement of lips to voice, but after a moment of conversation he tended to ignore it quite well. "You are the ones who brought in the Class-5 salvage?"

"That's right. I'm Kaylor Linn Todd and this is Adam Cain. He was cargo aboard the ship, and the only survivor."

Dess turned his attention to Adam. "Are you a slave?"

"Hell no!" Adam spat out, caught off guard by the question.

Kaylor placed a hand on Adam's arm. "There were eighty of his species aboard. You'll see in the survey that they were being transported in sophisticated hiberpods and in good condition, and definitely not as slaves."

Dess regarded them both for a moment, and then just grunted. He wrote something on a form in front of him. "How did you come upon the derelict?" he asked without looking up.

Kaylor knew he this was where he had to be careful. "We picked up the gravity wave in The Void and went to investigate. There were three pirate ships surrounding the derelict and they left the area as we came on scene."

Dess looked up. "They just left? You have a cargo hauler, don't you?"

"That's right. But we, ah, made ourselves out to be more than just a cargo hauler using some surplus satellite drones we had aboard. We didn't want to leave the ship to the mercy of the pirates. In The Void, all peaceful transports have to look out for one another. It just seemed like the right thing to do."

Again Dess grunted. "And you had nothing to do with the attack that disabled the ship and killed the inhabitants?"

"That's right. Adam here will testify to that."

Dess looked at Adam. "Is this your testimony?"

"All I know is that the ship I was on was attacked, and then after a battle onboard, the attackers left in a hurry. Later Kaylor showed up, by himself." Then Adam looked over at Kaylor. "And he saved my life."

"How is that?"

"I was the only one alive on the ship. If Kaylor had not chased off the pirates, they would have eventually found me, and I'd probably be dead by now, just like everyone else. Or if not that, then the power would have failed and I would have died from the cold or lack of atmosphere. Yeah, I guess he really did save my life."

Dess turned his attention back to Kaylor. "What were you doing that far out in The Void?"

"We were transporting a string of smokesticks to Rigor."

Dess nodded, and Adam got the distinct impression that he and Kaylor shared an unstated moment. Then the bureaucrat asked: "Have you removed anything from the subject vessel prior to registering the salvage with this authority?" It sounded like an official question.

"Nothing has been removed. I know the law."

Dess scribbled some more on the form, then punched a button on his desk. A keyboard rotated out of the top and Dess began to transcribe the information from his paper form into a computer. It took him several minutes to enter the data, during which he didn't say a word or acknowledge Adam and Kaylor's existence. Adam followed Kaylor's lead and sat patiently waiting for Dess to finish his job.

Finally, "The survey will be completed in about an hour. Return here at Day4 and we'll give you a copy and the registration documentation."

And that was it. The interview was over. But Adam wasn't done.

"Wait a minute. What about me? I need someone to take me back to Earth."

The bureaucrat stared back at Adam with a blank stare.

"Kaylor said you could get me back to my planet, to my home—"

"I said he *might* be able to." Kaylor interjected.

"Where are you from?" Dess asked.

"Earth, I'm from the planet Earth."

"Dirt? What kind of name is that for a planet?"

"Yeah, we've been through this before. Can you get me there or not?"

Dess tapped a few keys on his keypad. "Earth is rumored to be in the Far Arm," he said after scanning the screen for a moment. "I will stop right there. There is no one, official or otherwise, who can return you to a world in the Far Arm."

Adam felt as if an elephant had just sat on his chest. He broke out into a cold sweat and turned to Kaylor, pleading. "You said—"

"I'm sorry Adam. I told you the Far Arm is mostly unexplored territory. The computer doesn't even have a location for your homeworld. It would be impossible to find without specific coordinates."

"What would it take to get me to the Far Arm?"

"First of all, you would need a long-range starship, Class-5 or better, and then probably several million credits." Kaylor answered. "But y would need to know where you're going first, otherwise you'd spend a thousand years jumping from system to system until you found the right one. What is the lifespan of your species?"

Adam didn't like Kaylor's tone. He stood up, hovering over Kaylor. "A lot longer than yours if you keep feeding me your bullshit!"

"What was I supposed to tell you … that you're probably stuck here for the rest of your life with no chance of getting home? Would that have made you feel any better?"

Dess slapped his hand down on his desk, getting both of their attention. "Take this outside of my office. This subject has nothing to do with the Ministry."

Kaylor didn't thank the official, but instead quickly ushered Adam out of the room. Once in the hallway, Kaylor turned to him.

"You better come to terms with your situation, Adam Cain. *No one* is going to take you back to a planet with an unknown location, especially in the Far Arm."

"But I was abducted, kidnapped. It's not fair!"

"No, it's not, but this is not my problem."

"Then you should have left me on that ship—" He stopped suddenly and his eyes grew wide. *"The ship!"*

"What about it?"

"It's been to Earth."

"Yes, but the computer core is missing. There's no way to find where it's been."

"But the people who *own* the ship would know. The people who may come to claim it."

Kaylor was taken aback. He was right. If the ship *is* claimed, then Adam could talk with them about where its travels.

"Then you must stay here and wait to see if the ship is claimed," Kaylor declared.

"You mean you're not going to wait here yourself?"

"No. We'll come back later, if and when the claim is made."

Adam thought for a while. What would he do here if he stayed on Nimor? How would he survive? "You can't just leave me here. You said it could take a couple of months for the claim to come through. And what if no one ever comes to claim it?"

And that was exactly what Kaylor was hoping for. Then the entire ship would be his. He made a quick decision. "This is against my better judgment, but I'll let you stay with us, at least until the salvage is claimed or the salvage is awarded—if you cause us no more problems. Two months at the most. After that, you are on your own."

Adam didn't know whether to be happy or sad. It was obvious he wasn't getting home anytime soon, and he had no money and no profession in this alien universe. Yet he now found himself grasping for anything even remotely familiar. Staying with Kaylor and Jym would at least give him time to think, as well as acclimate himself to this strange, new universe. He nodded. "Thanks, Kaylor. I'm sorry I keep flying off the handle at you, but I'm pretty messed up right about now."

"I don't quite understand the phrasing," Kaylor said, "but I believe I understand what you mean to say. I can only imagine how strange all of this must seem to you. But if you attempt to remain calm, and stop *flying off the handle*, things will get better. Jym and I will help you get through."

Jym! How was Kaylor going to explain to him that Adam was going to be his new shipmate for the next two months? He's not going to like this ... not one little bit.

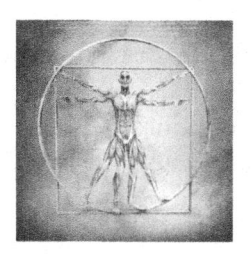

Chapter 10

Adam and Kaylor left the Ministry Compound and headed back into the rustic, Old West town just as the sun was setting. Kaylor explained that they could take one of the wheeled transports back to the spaceport, but first he wanted to stop by a favorite drinking establishment he knew of—a bar—and have a drink. Never one to pass up the opportunity to throw one back, Adam didn't resist.

Kaylor stopped at a doorway with a placard hung on a post, written in a scribble Adam couldn't even begin to decipher. Kaylor pulled open the door and quickly disappeared inside. Like a baby duckling, Adam followed.

The interior of the bar had such a foul odor that Adam almost gagged stepping inside—which was something he was coming to expect every time he came in contact with a new set of aliens. *It was as if none of them had a sense of smell!* The bar was dark inside, as was to be expected, and populated with a circus of creatures far more exotic and gritty-looking than the cantina scene from *Star Wars*. Also, there were no dancing girls or music playing, just the deafening cacophony of discordant alien voices and the clinking of glasses on wooden tables.

There was also a heavy haze in the room, and to Adam the smoke smelled vaguely familiar. But combined with alien sweat and breath, its pleasant scent was easily lost in the mix.

They took seats at a table near the center of the room with one of the small blood-sampling boxes affixed to its center. Kaylor poked his finger inside, pulled it out, and then rotated the box over to Adam. Without protest, Adam let the box take a sample. In a few moments, a waiter came over—another of the burly, hairy creatures—and Kaylor ordered a couple of drinks for the two of them.

Adam scanned the room, fascinated with the reality he now found himself in. Over in a far corner, he noticed a group of the skinny gray creatures like the ones he'd seen aboard the big ship—like the one who had initially yelled at him and then ended up fried during the battle. There were six of them, all huddled together, looking nervous.

Not too far way the tiny gray creatures was another group of patrons; four huge lizard-looking beings, all dressed in black leather and sporting bandoliers crossing their chests. Even from across the room, Adam could hear them carrying on, with numerous empty glasses filling the table before them. *There's some in every crowd,* Adam thought. *The loud-mouths, the arrogant drunks.*

Adam then noticed that Kaylor wasn't paying attention to any of this. His gaze was fixated on another creature seated at the bar, a being of a similar build as he, yet smaller and with smoother features. Adam watched as Kaylor's nostrils flared, sniffing the air.

"Stay here," Kaylor said as he lifted out of his chair and not looking at Adam as he did so. "I'll be back." He then proceeded to make a beeline for the bar.

Stunned and transfixed, Adam watched as the two creatures of the same species met for the first time and began to size each other up. It was all kind of creepy, as they first smelled each other up and down, and then began to rub their necks together, making contact with the inch-long fingers of skin dangling under their ears. Then the weirdest thing happened—Kaylor undid his pants! Then the female turned her back to him, while Kaylor grasped her waist and attempted to mount her—right there in the bar!

Almost immediately, the bartender came over and angrily yelled something to them. Frantically, the two of lovebirds hurried out the front door, leaving Adam sitting there alone, confused and more than a little embarrassed.

Holy crap! What was he supposed to do now, just sit there or follow?

Attempting to look as nonchalant as possible, Adam propped one arm up on the back of his chair and crossed his legs. When the bartender brought the drinks, Adam quickly snatched up his and took a long, healthy gulp. Expecting the cola-tasting drink like he'd had aboard Kaylor's ship, he was caught off guard by the unexpected burning sensation from the taste of very strong liquor. Tears erupted from his eyes, as the potent liquid blazed a trail all the way down to his stomach.

Adam tried his best not to choke; that would have completely destroyed the air of masculinity he was trying to project. Instead, he blinked several times and swallowed hard to dispel any linger traces of alcohol in his mouth. Once somewhat recovered, he then continued to scan the room as if nothing was wrong.

The lizard-like creatures in the corner caught his attention again, this time as a frail, rodent-looking thing passed too close to their table. The big lizard in the middle reached out and grabbed the rodent's tail and pulled, causing the big rat to fall into the group. They feigned anger and slapped at the rat's head several times before the biggest lizard kicked the rodent back into the room, sending him crashing into an empty table nearby. The other lizards laughed loudly and hysterically, cancelling out all other sounds in the room. Penitently, the abused rat rose to his feet, righted the table, and then scurried off without comment or a glance back at his tormentors.

It was then that Adam noticed that the big, dominate lizard was staring directly at him. Their eyes locked for a moment, before Adam looked away quickly. After a moment, he chanced a glance back, just to find that the lizard was still staring at him, a slight grin curling the edges of the creature's elongated snout. This was getting uncomfortable, especially without Kaylor around to narrate the scene.

So it was with infinite relief that Adam saw Kaylor reenter the tavern a few minutes later. When he was seated, Adam leaned forward, "What was *that* all about?"

The confused look returned Kaylor's face again. "You mean the mating? Doesn't your species mate?"

"Of course we do, but just not so fast, and in public—at least not all the time. Who was she?"

"I don't know," Kaylor said dismissively, lifting his drink and taking a gulp. "It doesn't matter. We see so few of our species out here that we need to take advantage of all encounters."

"So you just jump each other whenever you meet, just like that?"

"I don't see why you are so shocked. I'm sure that if another of your kind showed up you'd do the same."

Adam had to think about that for moment, but he was distracted from his thoughts when he noticed that the large lizard was still staring at him.

"Who are those lizard-things in the corner? One of them keeps looking at me."

Kaylor didn't look over as his voiced tensed. "They're Rigorians. I wouldn't mess with them if I were you. They're the meanest, strongest creatures in this part of the Fringe. Their clan is the largest and they know it."

"Yeah, they seem like real assholes."

"That's graphic, but accurate. Just be careful around them. They know they're the top of the food chain here, except, of course, for the Juireans."

Adam looked over at the lizard. Concerned that his furtive glances may be sending the wrong signal, Adam decided to try and disarm the situation, before it got out of hand.

Kaylor was still talking: "Whatever you do ..."

Adam flashed a big, toothy grin at the lizard—

"... don't ever bare your teeth at them. They will consider that a challenge."

Almost instantly, the big lizard jumped to his feet and stalked over to Adam's table. Towering a good seven feet tall, the yellow eyes and long snout were truly intimidating. Adam leaned back in his chair, looking up at the creature—as Kaylor nearly fell off his.

"You, creature," the Rigorian called out. "You challenge me?"

"Nah, it was just a misunderstanding," Adam blurted out, his voice cracking as he spoke.

"Yes, you challenge *me*. I therefore challenge *you*!"

The whole tavern fell silent as Adam carefully rose out of his seat, slowly so as to not spook the lizard any more than he already was. "Listen, I don't want to fight you. Like I said, it was just a misunderstanding."

The Rigorian placed his hand on the butt of this weapon, then noticing that Adam was unarmed, he cocked his head slightly toward Kaylor, never taking his eyes off of Adam. "Give him *your* weapon."

Adam was shocked to see Kaylor immediately start to unbuckle his holster and offer it to Adam. "What are you doing? I'm not going to fight this thing!"

"You've been challenged," Kaylor stated evenly. "You will either fight, or he has a right to shoot you dead where you stand."

So either I fight ... or I die. That's not much of a choice, Adam thought.

Taking a deep breath, Adam reluctantly took the holster and strapped it around his waist. At least this was something he was familiar with; a weapon and an enemy. This was basic. And this he was good at.

The lizard turned and walked back to his group as a path was cleared between the Rigorian and himself. There was more chatter in the room now, as the reality of the situation began to spread among the patrons. There even appeared to be some betting going on.

Adam moved out from behind the table, giving himself a clear line of sight to the Rigorian. Kaylor moved up beside him and removed the weapon from the holster. "Have you ever fired an MK-17 before?"

Adam shook his head.

"Of course you haven't." Kaylor showed him the weapon. "You must follow this procedure to fire the MK: Withdraw the weapon from the holster, bring it up to level, and when the targeting computer has locked on you will feel a slight vibration. You can then pull the trigger. This is set at level one. It's the maximum setting. It will produce a concentrated bolt but you will only have five shots per charge. It was set a level two when I shot you. That produced a larger, more diffused bolt, but it gives the shooter ten shots. You will need level one to kill the Rigorian, but you will also need to be very precise with your targeting."

He returned the weapon to the holster and then stepped away. Then as an afterthought, he stepped forward again and raised his arm. "This is *my* weapon," he announced to the room. "I will be reclaiming it after the challenge is satisfied."

Adam leaned toward him, "You don't sound too confident about my chances."

Kaylor just shrugged, and then put some more distance between Adam and himself.

Turning his attention to the Rigorian, Adam began to ask how this was supposed to go down when he saw the lizard's hand move toward his gun. The Rigorian grasped the butt of the weapon and began to draw it from the holster....

Oh shit! It's happening now.

Without thinking, Adam reached down and drew the MK-17. The weapon was light in his hand, and in a single move he aimed the weapon at the lizard and instinctively depressed the trigger. A tiny, brilliant ball of blue light shot out of the business end of the MK and impacted the left shoulder of the Rigorian, spinning him sideways. Adam fired again; this time the shot struck the thick neck of the lizard, nearly severing the head from the torso.

Adam then noticed another movement. The Rigorian to his right had pulled his own weapon and was bringing it to bear on Adam. Shifting his aim slightly, Adam let loose with another shot, one that found its target center mass in the lizard's chest.

Not taking any chances, Adam swung the weapon to the left, lining up the other two Rigorians in his sights. Each had their hands on their weapons, but they quickly pulled them away as they stared down the barrel of Adam's gun.

It was only then that Adam felt a slight vibration coming from the MK-17.

For some reason, this made him chuckle. The entire fight had taken less than two seconds, and just *now* the computer was telling him it was okay to fire.

"Take off your holsters," Adam demanded of the two remaining Rigorians.

"What?" one of them said. "We're not taking—"

Adam rushed forward, jamming the barrel of his gun up into the neck of the taller, defiant lizard. "Take off your goddamn weapons—or I'll take off your head!"

In unison, the Rigorians unbuckled their holsters and let them fall to the floor.

"That's better. Now get the hell out of here," Adam ordered.

Without looking at the fallen and bloody heap of flesh that was their dead companions, the two surviving Rigorians dashed out of the tavern. Adam bent down and picked up the two sets of weapons. When he turned back to the room, he noticed how deathly quiet it was, with dozens of pairs of eyes staring widely back at him. Taking advantage of the stunned fear, Adam returned to his table, lifted his drink and threw it down in a single gulp. He then turned to an equally stunned Kaylor and simply said, "Pay up; we're leaving."

Outside in the early evening afterglow, Adam and Kaylor walked silently back to the spaceport. Kaylor had not asked for his weapon back, and actually stayed about a half-pace behind Adam all the way back.

Entering the ship, Kaylor retracted the ramp loading and secured the door, after which they made their way to the common room.

Upon entering, Jym turned from his computer console—and nearly fell off the chair at the sight of Adam.

"What is *he* doing here?" he blurted, but Kaylor silenced him up with a firm shake of his head.

Adam was still so jacked up that he didn't sit down. He dropped the two sets of weapons on the table and then paced back and forth between the couch and the table. "I didn't want to fight him; you know that," he finally said.

Kaylor stood near the doorway. "You had no choice," was all he said.

Regaining some nerve, Jym pressed the subject: "What happened? You've only been gone for about two hours—"

"Adam just killed two Rigorians in a challenge at Jklena's Tavern."

"He *what*? That's impossible."

"No it's not. It was the most remarkable thing I've ever seen. And then he disarmed two more and then kicked them out of the bar."

Stepping forward, Kaylor held out his hand toward Adam. "Let me have the weapon."

Adam stopped pacing and looked straight into Kaylor's eyes. A tense moment passed, and then slowly Adam began to unbuckle the holster. "No keep the holster on," Kaylor said.

Surprised, Adam obeyed and handed over just the weapon. Taking the MK-17, Kaylor popped the bolt cartridge out of the handle and then handed the weapon back to Adam.

"Let me see you draw the weapon again. It's disarmed. Just draw and shoot, like you did before."

Doing his best John Wayne imitation, Adam whipped the gun out of the holster, raised it and pulled the trigger. He heard an audible gasp from Jym.

"What's the big deal?" Adam asked. "I've always had pretty fast reactions. And I'm actually a damned good shot."

After a moment, Kaylor answered. "You should not be able to do that. I've never seen anyone even come close to how fast you can draw a weapon. Also, you didn't use the targeting computer. How is it that you can hit a target without targeting assistance?"

"Well, that part seemed pretty stupid to me. Why do you have to wait for a computer to tell you when to shoot?"

Kaylor persisted. "You should not be able to hit a target without assistance. If you do, then it is pure luck. But what I saw today was not luck."

"Sorry to disappoint you, but we don't use targeting computers on our handguns. We do with missiles and rockets and things like that, but not with handguns or rifles. Besides, he was only about twenty feet away. I'd have to be blind to miss at that range."

Jym coughed. "I don't mean to spoil this moment, but what about the salvage?"

Kaylor seemed relieved at the change the subject. "It's registered. We are to go back tomorrow at Day4 for the final inventory and receipt."

"And him?" Jym nodded toward Adam, who was still practicing drawing the MK-17, seemingly getting faster every time.

"The Registrar said he couldn't help him get back to Earth, so I said he could stay on with us until the owners showed up for the claim or the verdict on the salvage is rendered. He's hoping that if the owners show up they could help him find his home."

"But that could be months or more. You mean he's going to be here all that time?"

"I told him two months—"

"Hey, I'm right here in the room with you," Adam said.

"We'll put him to work, doing something. But I wasn't about to leave him on-planet without any resources."

"It looks like he can take care of himself," Jym countered.

"If killing is an occupation…."

Adam turned toward the two arguing aliens: "Listen, I'm not going to be any trouble for you. I'm a hard worker and a fast learner, and I appreciate everything you've done for me. But I just need a little time to figure out what I'm going to do." He took a few steps towards Jym. "Remember, from my perspective, it was only about a day ago that I was back home, without ever having dreamed I'd be here going through all this shit. This is *your* reality, not mine. So Jym, why don't you cut me a little slack!"

Jym had recoiled from Adam as the diatribe grew more impassioned. Now he recovered slightly. "That's understandable. I'm just not used to someone disturbing our routine. If it's okay with Kaylor, then it's okay with me."

"That's better," Adam said forcefully. "Now can we all just try to get along?" And with that, Adam took off the holster and handed it back to Kaylor. He then gathered up the two other weapons he'd taken from the Rigorians and left to return to his room. He had a lot of thinking to do....

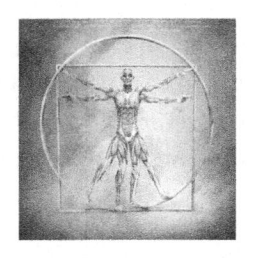

Chapter 11

Overlord Oplim Ra Unis was having a terrible day. He had just received a report that tax revenues for The Fringe were down seventeen-percent and that the mining operations on Castor were stalled because of a delay in getting a new drilling unit shipped in from the Seventh Sector.

But what frustrated the young Overlord the most was that his superiors back on Juir would not care. To them, The Fringe was so inconsequential, such an afterthought, that they treated the region as a bonus to all their other operations. No matter what Oplim did, he would never be noticed.

And that was why so many of his colleagues in the Juirean Authority had been shocked to learn that Oplim had actually *requested* The Fringe. With such a vast and growing Expansion, and so few Juireans available to fill vital posts, he could have had his pick of any of a dozen Sectors. Yet he chose The Fringe.

Oplim closed the file on his computer, leaned back in his chair and stared out through the huge plate glass window that made up the entire right wall of his office. The city of Cyol on the planet Melfora Lum was where the Juireans had established their sector headquarters some seventy-odd standard years before. It was the largest city in The Fringe, as would be expected, with skyscrapers and traffic routes, even elevated arrow trains that shuttled the inhabitants to and from their tasks. The planet itself offered a temperate climate, ample farmland, and even the gravity was nearly that of Juir. But it had been Oplim's hobby—indeed his obsession—that had brought him to Melfora Lum, and out to the very edge of the civilized galaxy.

So when his secure computer link buzzed and he opened the file, his heart began to race rapidly, as his breath came in shallow gulps.

Could this be it? Could this be what he came all the way out here to find?

Oplim had traces on all communications throughout The Fringe, including vidcasts, link transmissions, ship registrations—and even salvages. Search parameters were entered and any hits, even the most obscure, were correlated and weighed against all known databases.

This hit came from a salvage that had just been registered on the planet Nimor. Undoubtedly, Oplim had received the information only milliseconds behind even the bureaucrats on Nimor. But unlike them, Oplim was privy to information they were not.

The configuration was correct, the technology consistent, and even the dead occupants coincided with the archives. This was definitely a *Klin* ship. At last he had his proof!

For over twenty standard years, Oplim had tracked every credible sighting, report, rumor or myth regarding the Klin. Within his program, he had noted each of these, no matter how vague, and soon a pattern had begun to emerge.

As The Expansion grew larger, the locations of the most recent reports would move inexorably further out, away from the more populated regions of the galaxy. It was obvious what was happening: The Klin were moving. And now there was no place further out than The Fringe.

It had been a remarkable gamble on Oplim's part. After all, many in The Expansion did not even believe that the Klin still existed, and to be labeled a Believer did not sit well with the Elites or the Juirean Council. Besides, with a whole galaxy to govern, most Juireans did not have the time or inclination to pursue fairy tales. The Klin had been eradicated during *The Reckoning*. They no longer existed as a race.

And yet here was a *Klin* ship—in the flesh.

Oplim watched the video that the survey crew had taken. Even though the ship itself was not conclusive evidence—after all, it had been nearly four-thousand years since anyone had seen a Klin spaceship—it was the bodies they found onboard that cinched it. Evolution does not work so fast that in four-thousand years a species would not be recognizable. The Juireans had plenty of records that showed what a Klin looked like, even though it had been four millennia since anyone had verifiably seen one in the flesh, even a dead one.

But just finding hard evidence that the Klin still existed wasn't enough for Oplim. The Klin had to have a base of operations somewhere, and more-than-likely, it was right here in his sector.

Oplim quickly scanned the report until he found what he was looking for. He slammed his fist down hard on his desk! He was afraid of this—the ship's computer core was missing. That core would hold the location to the Klin hiding place.

Reading quickly, Oplim saw where it was reported that the damn Fringe Pirates had attacked the ship and then removed certain items, including the core, before abandoning their kill. He read with admiration—and a little humor—how a pair of lowly mule-drivers had tricked the pirates into running away. Unfortunately, before they left, they had taken the core.

But wait, what was this? He read further. There was a survivor! Not a Klin, but another creature who had been aboard the Klin ship. The vids were both informative and confusing. There had been 80 of these creatures—*Humans* they were called—and they had all been intentionally killed by the Klin, all except for one. And he was on Nimor.

Oplim's mind quickly assessed the situation and then formulated a plan, as Overlords had been trained to do for thousands of years.

Tapping the communications tab on his desk, he commanded that a secure and direct link be established between himself and Fleet Commander Giodol Fe Bulen.

Commander Giodol was surprised to be receiving a link directly from the Overlord. He answered immediately.

"Commander, where are you at this time?"

"We are near Silea, My Lord, showing our force to the natives," he answered. With no real enemies in this part of The Expansion, the tiny Fringe fleet was used primarily for intimidation purposes, as a reminder of just how powerful the Juireans were.

"I have a vital assignment for you," Oplim stated. Giodol seemed to perk up. He was so tired of simply "showing the flag" to these backwater beings. "I need you to launch an assault the pirate base at K'ly and extract information from all the captives."

Giodol was stunned. Was he hearing his Overlord correctly? This was *real* action, and against the only menace—if minor—within the region. The Fleet Commander knew that recently the pirates had become much bolder and proficient with their activities, actually staging raids on planetary cities. They also appeared to be working better as a unit, rather than as independent ships with no real organization. Now the young Overlord was finally going to take action against them. "Of course, My Lord, I will do as you wish with enthusiasm. It's time we subdue the pirate activities—"

The Overlord continued, interrupting: "Yesterday, a ship was attacked by three pirate ships in The Void, near the planet Nimor. The pirates made off with the ship's computer core. That is what you must recover."

Giodol was surprised by the assignment. This was something different than punishment for the pirates' sector-wide crimes.

"Commander, you are authorized to use whatever means necessary to recover the core."

"Was it removed from a Juirean ship, My Lord?" Giodol asked, trying to find the reason why this particular core would be so important to the Overlord.

"No, it was not. But that is not your concern. Just bring me the core as soon as it is recovered." Then the Overlord broke the link.

Giodol stared at the blank screen for a few more seconds, wondering why the Overlord was acting so strangely. Oplim had come to The Fringe only two years before, while Giodol had been there for nearly ten. He had experienced no issues with the young Overlord until this time, and even now, this was not an issue he would dwell on. The Overlord must have his reasons. *And we're Juireans; we never question the motives of another Juirean.*

Giodol knew the location of the pirate base on K'ly; it was one of the least kept secrets in The Fringe. It's just that no one had ever taken the initiative to go there before. Now he had a mission, a purpose. And as he had told the Overlord, he would accomplish his assignment with enthusiasm.

After breaking the link with his Fleet Commander, Oplim next opened a link to Counselor Deslor Lin Jul on Castor. Deslor was one of three Counselors assigned to the Overlord, but by far his favorite. He also shared Oplim's belief in the existence of the Klin.

Once the link was established, Oplim spent the first few minutes briefing Deslor regarding the Klin ship and the actions he'd set in motion against the Fringe Pirates. The Counselor, too, was ecstatic.

"Deslor, I need you to go to Nimor and interview the mule-drivers. They are not to spread any information regarding this ship, is that clear?"

"Perfectly," Deslor said. "I assume you have put a lock on all references to the ship and its recovery?"

"Of course. And then I want you to bring the ship—and this survivor—to me here on Melfora Lum. As far as we can tell, this creature has had direct contact with the Klin. We must know the connection between the Klin and ..." he looked down at his notes, "... these Humans. How soon can you get to Nimor?"

"I can be there in seventeen hours."

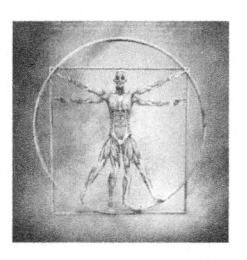

Chapter 12

The next morning, Adam learned that *Day 4* meant four hours after sunrise on Nimor. Everyone seemed to be in a better mood this morning, even Jym, as the three of them crowded into a "cab" for the trip to the Ministry Compound.

There was a marked increase in activity at the Compound this morning compared to the day before, with literally dozens of the hairy creatures scurrying about with obvious purpose. Adam thought that yesterday they'd just hit the place right around closing time....

It doesn't really matter, he thought. Today was the day he would begin his journey home, optimistic that the ship's owners would soon come to claim their property.

As he sat in the back of transport, he proudly displayed the MK-17 bolt launcher he wore on his hip. He'd even found a strand of leather in the cargo hold which he used to tie the bottom of the holster to his lower thigh, just to keep it from riding up when he drew the weapon. This had allowed him to quicken his draw even more. He felt much better wearing the weapon in this strange, new environment. As a military man, his weapon was his best friend.

In addition, Adam carried with him a slight superiority complex, based on the reactions he'd witnessed from Kaylor and Jym the day before. They made him believe that he'd actually accomplished something pretty spectacular against the yellow-eyed lizards. It also meant that if this was the best these aliens had to throw at him, then he really had nothing much to worry about.

As a matter of fact, Adam kept playing the fight scene over and over again in his mind, and each time he did, he realized that he had never been in any real danger from the lizard-things. The speed of their draws was like watching it in slow motion. And even if they had equaled him in drawing speed, they would have stood there for a second or so before ever firing, while the damn targeting computer did its thing.

Was this how they all did it? If so...well damn!

Adam followed Kaylor and Jym as they entered the brick building once again and took the stairs to the second floor. The building was packed, but the office of Fredic Dess was empty, except for the ubiquitous bureaucrat.

Dess was especially friendly this morning, much more cordial than the day before. But he did start the conversation with an apology. "I'm terribly sorry, but I must insist that you remove your weapons and place them on the table over there." He indicated a table set against the left wall, next to the second door to his office. "We have a dignitary arriving today and we have instituted new restrictions for today only."

Even though Adam was just getting used to his new sidearm, he obliged, as did Kaylor; Jym was not carrying a weapon.

Once they were all seated in front of the desk, Dess leaned back in his chair and locked his gaze on Adam. Suddenly, seven black-vested guards burst into the room from both entrances, each pointing their long-barrel weapons at Adam. Adam jumped up from his seat, but after a quick survey of the situation, he sank back into the chair with a resigning sigh.

"You, the Human known as Adam Cain, are to be detained pending investigation of the unprovoked murder of two Rigorian primes yesterday late day," Dess announced to him.

"That was self-defense." Kaylor countered, much to his credit. Adam remained silent, surveying the armed guards.

"That is not what the witnesses relay. A Council will be convened to weigh all the evidence."

Adam leaned over closer to Kaylor. "I thought you said there wasn't much law around here."

"I was there." Kaylor said, ignoring Adam. "The Rigorians initiated the challenge. It was a fair fight."

"Two Rigorian warriors, dead in a challenge with a single being?" Dess shook his head. "I'm not a judge here, but I find that hard to believe. He will be held within the Compound as we investigate."

It was then that Kaylor noticed the guards were also pointing their weapons at he and Jym. "What are you doing—?"

Dess cut him off. "And the two of you are to be detained as well, pending the arrival of and questioning by Juirean Counselor Deslor Lin Jul."

Adam saw the look of shock on the faces of his two companions, a blood-draining mask of terror different from any previous expressions Adam had witnessed. This was different. This was pure fright.

"A Juirean Counselor is coming here—to see *us*?"

"That is correct. The Juirean Authority has taken over the case of your salvage. It is no longer under local jurisdiction."

Kaylor started to say something before nearly choking. Once he regained his voice, he asked, "When will the Counselor be arriving?"

"He will be here later today, approximately Day10. You will be held here until his arrival."

"But we haven't done anything wrong."

"Immaterial. I am only following orders."

"But we're not going anywhere. Why can't we leave and return when he arrives?"

"That is not my decision to make. Take them away."

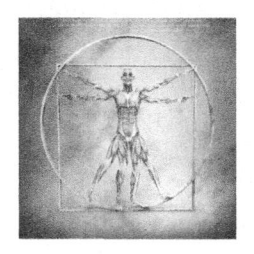

Chapter 13

Riyad Tarazi had just finished a rigorous workout when the link came through from Angar in Gildemont. Bare-chested, he wrapped a towel around his shoulders and opened the link.

"What do you have to report?"

Angar was seated before a computer screen in what appeared to be a planetside room, not aboard his ship. "The Ministry has completed their survey, and the computer core is *not* on the ship. The report says the *pirates* took it." His tone was incredulous.

"Well, seeing that it was *your* crew that went aboard, do *you* have it?"

"No, sir! Absolutely not!" Angar cried in his defense. "We didn't have time to do any salvage before—well—before we left."

"Then the bastard mule-driver must have it."

"The report indicates that his ship passed a cursory inspection."

"He wouldn't keep it on his ship. He probably took other things as well."

Angar looked down at a screen in front of him. "Yes, there were several small units missing, but again, all supposedly taken by us."

"He would have hidden them somewhere along the way to Nimor." Then the obvious answer popped into his head. "The asteroids. He hid the core there."

"There are millions of them, sir."

"Yes, I know. That's why we need to get the driver to tell us where he hid the core. Where is the bastard now?"

"They are being detained at the Ministry."

"Detained? Why?"

The blood seemed to drain from Angar's face. "They are awaiting the arrival of a Juirean Counselor for interrogation"

Juireans! Why did they care about this salvage?

"When will the Counselor be arriving?"

"Very soon. The Ministry is making arrangements for the interrogation of the two mule-drivers, and of the one survivor."

"Survivor? *What survivor?*" Riyad was upset that this was the first he was hearing of this.

"Yes, there seems to have been one survivor." Realizing his mistake, almost all the blood rushed from Angar's face. "One of the beings from the hiberpods is still alive."

"A Human is still alive? Why wasn't I told of this?" Riyad literally leaped out of his chair. The facial recognition sensor on the vid camera followed his movement, and kept him on screen with Angar.

"Apologies, My General. When we went aboard there were dozens of hiberpods. All the creatures were dead, except this one, evidently."

Riyad stared at the captain for several long moments, while Angar shifted nervously, waiting for Riyad to continue.

Finally, Riyad spoke. "Where is this survivor now?" His speech was slow and cadenced.

"He, too, is being detained at the Ministry. But he is being held pending a murder investigation."

This was the last thing Riyad had expected to hear. "What do you mean? Explain yourself."

"Early the prior evening, the survivor apparently killed two Rigorians in a life challenge. Witnesses say it was unprovoked, that's how two of them could be killed by a single creature."

That's not so unbelievable, not in light of what I've just been told, Riyad thought. *Another live Human being, and it didn't take long for his abilities to manifest themselves.* But that information he would have to deal with later. Right now he had a more urgent matter.

"Captain Angar, I'm giving you the most important task of your life. Fail this, and you will not have a life left to live." Angar swallowed hard, his eyes wide with fear and anticipation. "The mule-drivers must be freed from the Nimorians—alive—and brought to me. If the driver is killed, with him will go the location of the computer core I seek. You can use any of our contacts in the Clans and in the Ministry to secure their release. Do what you must. And one last thing," his voice lowered slightly, "if you cannot subdue the survivor without risking the lives of the mule-drivers, then you must kill him. Is that clear?"

"Yes, sir! I already have a major contact in the Ministry. I begin organizing for the rescue as soon as possible."

"Keep me informed of your progress." Riyad cut the link.

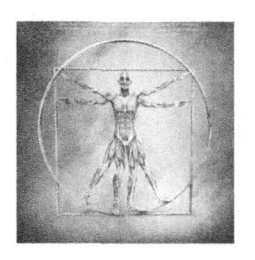

Chapter 14

Well this is just great, Adam thought, as he led the parade out of the office and down the stairs.

The jail block was located in the next building over, and as they made their way there, Adam tried to think if there was any way out of his current situation. Again, being on an alien planet took away most of his options. Even if he could escape, where would he go? He knew he was innocent of the charges against him; after all, he had killed the lizards in a fair fight. So as they approached the four-story brick building, Adam decided he'd just let things ride and see played out, even though he had no idea how fair was alien justice.

Solid metal doors greeted them at the prison building, and they entered into a processing room with high counters manned by grim-looking natives wearing tan vests instead of the black ones the guards wore. The three detainees were herded through another security gate made of thin metal bars and taken down a wide corridor to a series of jail cells.

The familiarity of the cells once again amazed Adam. About the only thing that made this scene alien were the creatures escorting him. The room itself was long, with ten cells along the right side. Each cell was lined with the same thin metal bars as the security door, running up from the floor to the ceiling with no parallel supports joining them, and they were open to each other except for a wall of bars separating them. Inside each cell were two cots, one placed along each side wall of the cell, and with a sink and toilet set along the solid back wall. There were no windows to the outside. Adam, Kaylor and Jym were the only occupants in the cell block.

Adam was placed in one cell, while Kaylor and Jym were placed together in another. Once the gates were locked, the guards left.

Adam walked over to the sink and splashed some water on his face. Looking around, he found no towel, so he pulled up the sheet up on one of the cots and dried off. Then he sat on the cot facing the cell of his alien companions, where the two of them were in an animated, yet hushed conversation.

"Hey," Adam called out to them, "what just happened in there?"

Kaylor and Jym ignored him.

"Hey, alien dudes!" This time he got their attention. "What are you two so excited about? You're not the one accused of murder."

"Don't worry about that," Kaylor said dismissively. "I'm sure they'll get it all worked out once they interview more of the witnesses from the tavern." He then turned back to him conversation with Jym.

Adam decided to use a different tact. "So what's a Juirean Counselor?"

This got both of their attention.

Kaylor moved closer to the bars separating the two cells. "Didn't I tell you the Juireans rule the civilized galaxy? Having a Juirean come here, to meet us—well there must be something very special about that ship I found you on."

"That's not my area of expertise. Remember, I was just *cargo*."

Kaylor looked annoyed, while Jym settled on the far away cot and sat down. "You don't understand how serious this is," Kaylor said. "The Juirean Expansion encompasses over eight-thousand stellar systems. Juireans don't bother themselves with every little thing that goes on within them, especially not way out here in The Fringe. I've been out in this part of The Expansion for almost twenty standard years, and I've never even *seen* a Juirean in person."

"I saw one once," Jym interjected. "But it was at a big celebration on my homeworld, and it was from pretty far away."

Kaylor ignored the interruption. "A Counselor is only one step below an Overlord, and the only other level above that are the Elites—but they never leave Juir. I've heard that there are only about ten Juireans in the entire Fringe. Do you see now why we are so concerned?"

"I guess so. But you didn't do anything wrong, either. So relax. It will all work itself out," Adam offered, with a trace of sarcasm in his voice.

Kaylor placed both his hands on the cell bars, favoring his broken left arm, and hung his head slightly. "It also looks like they may take away our salvage."

Adam could tell that the two aliens were really worried. "So, tell me more about these Juireans. How did they come to be the top dogs in the galaxy?"

Adam's reference to "top dogs" seemed to confuse Kaylor for a moment, as he appeared to be listening to the translator work through the reference. Then he sat on the cot and leaned back against the bars at the front of the cell.

"I have to say, the Juireans are not to be taken lightly. They control the technology and manufacturing capacity of The Expansion. They also have the strongest weapons and largest fleets. They're the ones who have tied the entire known galaxy together. Their Expansion reaches from the other side of the Core, to this side of the galaxy and on to The Fringe, at the edge of the Far Arm—the place where you apparently come from. There's still a lot of galaxy to explore, and eventually the Juireans will control it all."

"That doesn't answer the question about *how* they did it."

"That goes back about four-thousand years ago, and to the Seven World Common Alliance." Kaylor began. Adam could tell this line of conversation was helping Kaylor take his mind off of his current situation. It was doing the same for Adam....

"The way it all began, according to the stories, was within a small stellar cluster with four dominate stars, and around them orbited seven habitable worlds. This was long before interstellar travel and gravity drives. In certain times during their orbits, most of these planets would come very near to one another, near enough that powerful telescopes could pick up the lights on their surfaces and other signs of intelligent life. As each species evolved, their primary purpose became to make contact with their neighboring planets.

"Again, according to the stories, science and technology advanced very quickly on these worlds, as they bypassed the normal beliefs in religion and such that most other civilizations hold to be true. With the natives of these planets knowing from the very beginning that there were beings on their neighboring worlds, the belief in one god—or in even their own uniqueness based on some divine creation—was an obsolete concept. My own homeworld of Belson—as well as most of the others I've visited—still hold onto these ancient religious beliefs, even to this day. Studies have shown that such superstitions and restrictions tend to slow the progress of science by thousands of years.

"But not so in the Alliance. While we were riding steeds and building our first wheeled carts, some of the races in the Alliance were already building rockets and developing wave transmitters in an attempt to communicate with the other worlds of the cluster.

"So in a relatively short time, some of these races began traveling back and forth between planets and sharing technology. The Klin, the Diphorians and the Oanneans were some of the first, establishing the rudimentary Alliance. They eventually set criteria for entry into their organization, the most important of which was that each planet must be united under one government before they would be offered full membership in the Alliance.

"The Juireans, according to these stories, were still divided and tribal at this time, yet they, too, knew of the beings on their neighboring worlds and wanted to join them. But the other worlds considered them too barbaric and warlike for membership. This made the Juireans mad. In fact, at that time, the planet where the Juireans come from was called Axlus, and it was made up of hundreds of city-states, with the city-state of Juir being just one of them.

"But then a leader arose on Axlus, a Juirean named Malor the Great, who began a concerted effort to unify the planet. After a long and bloody campaign, he eventually succeeded, and he changed the name of the planet to Juir. When he was done, The Others—as they were called—arrived."

Kaylor stretched, giving himself some relief from the hard metal bars against his back. Then seeing that Adam was actually paying attention to his lecture, he continued.

"By then, the Alliance consisted of six of the seven worlds in the cluster. Even though Juir was united now, they were still not granted full membership in the Alliance. The other civilizations still considered them too violent and belligerent. This caused an incredible amount of anger within the Juirean population, since they had killed millions of their own kind just to bring about the unification that had been required for membership. But Malor devised a plan to remedy this.

"At the time, the Klin and the Oanneans were in a minor struggle for control of the Alliance, and Malor convinced the Klin that the Juireans could use their more militaristic abilities to provide protection and security for the Klin, a race who had never had to fight before, either among themselves or against others. So the

Juireans were eventually granted full membership in the Alliance and given complete access to all the technology the coalition had to offer. This was a mistake—but not if you listen to the Juireans tell it."

Adam could tell from the tone of Kaylor's story that he had no love lost for the Juireans. Yet Adam was finding the story fascinating. Here was a tale of *real* galactic conquest by *real* aliens. This was better than any movie or sci-fi book.

Kaylor continued.

"Juireans live for a very long time, often a couple of hundred years or more. And over the fifty years or so since Malor had unified the planet—and they were still denied membership in the Alliance—the Juireans had developed an intense hatred for the other members of the Alliance, especially the Klin, whom they held responsible for this insult. So once Malor and the Juireans gained access to the Alliance technology, including the newly-developed gravity drive for interstellar travel, they attacked.

"To the Juireans, this is a time of immense pride and accomplishment in their history. To this day they still celebrate *The Reckoning*, as they call it. Throughout the cluster, the Juireans decimated the other races, who, similar to the Klin, had never developed an advanced military or fighting skills equal to the Juireans. Yet the Juireans focused the brunt of their revenge on the Klin. They sterilized the Klin homeworld and exterminated the race."

"Not all of them!" Jym finally spoke up.

"What do you mean?" Adam asked.

Kaylor answered for him. "What he means is that there are accounts—rumors really—that some of the Klin escaped and went into hiding. The tales say that the Klin will someday rise again and vanquish the Juireans and reclaim the Alliance as their own."

"You don't believe that?"

"It's been almost four thousand years and there has never been any verifiable proof that the Klin still exist."

"They've been to Fulqin!" Jym countered.

"Fulqin is Jym's homeworld," Kaylor explained. "Nearly every race has their myths." He turned to Jym, "Admit it Jym, no one has actually produced a real Klin for the transmissions, now have they?"

"They're just being cautious."

"Go on," Adam said to Kaylor.

"Once the Juireans had conquered the Alliance, they set out bringing other worlds under their control using the new gravity drive. But soon wars were breaking out all over the place, and the Juireans found themselves assaulted on all sides.

"By this time Malor had died, and the Juireans went through a series of ineffective leaders until Arolus Ra Un came to power. He was a strong and fearless leader who decided that the best way to bring unity to the warring factions of the Alliance was to give them all a new purpose, something new to fight against, other than themselves. So he built The Mass."

"What was that?" Adam asked.

"As the name suggests, it was a *massive* fleet of 10,000 starships that fanned out in all directions across the galaxy, conquering worlds through force, intimidation or by politics. Some races resisted, but none were able to hold out for long. The Mass lasted for five hundred years, until it became so large and unmanageable that the Juireans had to stop to catch their breath. By this time, the lust for power by the Juireans was fairly well-exhausted, and they found that the task of governing all the worlds of the new Alliance was almost too much to bear.

"So they retreated briefly, letting thousands of systems fall back to their pre-contact existences. As it turned out, this caused more harm than good. Once most of these worlds had experienced the wonders of the Juirean technology—stolen from the Klin, I might add—they longed for more. So they fought regional wars for what was left by the Juireans. I know this to be true, because my homeworld was involved in one of the bloodiest and most protracted of these wars."

"So what happened next? Obviously the Juireans didn't stay quiet for long."

"No, they didn't," Kaylor agreed. "They came out with a new strategy: The Expansion. Realizing that a galaxy is too big for one race to control, the Juireans allowed regional alliances, as well as individual planets to petition for entry into The Expansion, yet retain a high level of autonomy and self-rule. Through this strategy they were able to gain control over thousands of additional worlds by giving the local authorities more freedom, in exchange for allegiance and a tribute paid to the Juireans. And the strongest of these local authorities gained access to the most technology the Juireans allowed them to have.

"Yet the Juireans had learned from their past. To this day, they maintain strict control of the technology, only doling out bits and pieces, and never the means of production. In fact, the Juirean culture these days is built almost entirely on managing their Expansion and the manufacture of the technology."

"Sounds like a pretty reasonable thing to do," Adam said. "These Juireans don't sound that bad." As soon as Adam finished his statement, the look of disgust on the faces of the two aliens told him he didn't have all the facts.

"How can you say that?" Kaylor asked, scorn in his voice. "The Juireans are heartless animals who only have what they've got by stealing it from others."

"Sorry," Adam said. "It just kinda made sense. How else are you going to govern a whole galaxy?"

Kaylor just shook his head, a dismissive gesture toward someone who knew no better. Then he continued: "Since they are only one race, the Juireans insist that the ultimate authority in The Expansion is always left to a Juirean. So they have breeding factories; they don't have traditional mating pairs like most races. Children are analyzed for ability, and then separated at an early age to be trained to perform various tasks within the Juirean structure.

"Like I said, at the very top of their hierarchy are the Elites, followed by the Overlords and then the Counselors. Below them are the various administrators and technicians. The Overlords run the governors of The Expansion, along with the Guards, who run the military side of the society. But the Juireans are the sole arbiters of their actions. No other race, except for other Juireans, can even question the decisions of an Overlord. The Counselors are more of the regional administrators, answerable only to the local Overlord. Located at the very edge of The Expansion, The Fringe has very few Juireans of any classification. We just aren't that important to them."

"And that's why you're so concerned about this Counselor coming today?" Adam said. "I can see that drawing the attention of a Juirean, let alone a Juirean Counselor, must mean there's something very strange about that spaceship I was on."

Kaylor just bobbed his head, yet it didn't take an alien body language expert to read the worry on his face. Finally Kaylor asked Adam, "And you know nothing more about the ship or where it came from?"

"How could I?" Adam answered. "You know I come from some backwater world that doesn't even have space travel—not real space travel like you have. Hell, we've only been to our own moon a few times. I honestly have no idea where the ship came from, or why I was even aboard."

"But there were a total of eighty of your race in the pods. That must mean something?" Jym said from the faraway cot.

"Hell if I know. Remember, to me I've only been awake in your universe for about two days, and already I've fought with you," he pointed at Kaylor, "been in a gunfight with two crazed lizards, and been arrested for murder. To top that off, back home they probably think I'm dead, and all the people I know and love have already put me six-feet under. Damn, this adventure is getting off to a great start! I wonder what tomorrow will bring?"

Kaylor grunted. "At least you don't have to face a Counselor."

"That may be true, but you do realize now that my chances of meeting the owners of that ship are virtually nonexistent? And if that's the case, then I'm truly fucked!" With that Adam slammed his hand hard against a bar of the cell—and was shocked to see that it had bent outward about an inch!

Looking over quickly to see if Kaylor or Jym had noticed, he was relieved to see that they hadn't. Shifting on the cot until he was seated like Kaylor, with his back against the front bars, Adam stretched out his legs on the cot. He then placed his left foot against another bar of the cell, and using the bars at his back as a backstop, pushed with his leg. With some effort, he felt the bar begin to give.

He stopped, and once more looked over at the two aliens. Jym had fallen back on his cot, while Kaylor was staring straight ahead toward the rear of the cell, lost in thought. Adam didn't know why he wanted to keep his latest discovery a secret from them, but he felt he had to. He had no doubt, that if he wanted to, he could separate the bars enough to slip through. Of course, the bars on this side of the cell simply lead to another cell, but he knew he could bend the front ones just as easily.

Now that he knew he *could* escape, he was at a loss as to what to do with this knowledge. This whole planet—hell this entire alien universe—was a prison for him. Without a plan, he was still screwed. And he didn't have enough knowledge or experience to formulate a workable one.

What to do? What to do?

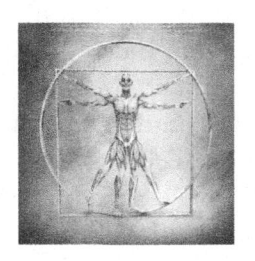

Chapter 15

The next few hours passed without much interaction between the three prisoners, but they all sat up when they heard a commotion coming from the processing room. The door to the cell block opened suddenly and a flood of creatures began to enter.

Kaylor and Jym jumped to their feet, while Adam remained seated on his cot.

About a dozen of the natives entered the cell block, followed by five of the mean-looking lizard creatures Adam knew to be Rigorians, like the ones he'd killed the night before.

After the lizards, the Juirean entered. Adam reasoned it had to be the Juirean because of the deference granted him, as well as the fact that he was about a foot taller than anyone else in the room, including the seven-foot tall Rigorians. Adam quickly noticed, however, that a lot of the Counselor's added height came from his magnificent mane of hair. It flowed from his wide forehead and puffed out on top for a good foot, before cascading halfway down his back. The hair was a pale yellow color, which stood out in stark contrast to the creature's swarthy complexion. The hair framed face, which tapered down from the wide forehead, past a simple, normal looking nose and smallish mouth, to culminate at a pencil-thin chin thrusting out from the jaw line.

Adam couldn't tell much about the creature's build, since he was draped in several layers of flowing capes of greens, blues and reds. It was all quite the spectacle.

Still, Adam wasn't that impressed.

The Juirean Counselor, Deslor Lin Jul, stepped closer to the bars of Kaylor and Jym's cell and took a screenpad from one of the Nimorians. After scanning the screen, he locked his steely gaze upon Kaylor. "You are the salvager?" His voice was extremely strong and projecting; Adam reasoned that came from centuries of being at the top of the food chain throughout much of the galaxy. *Having that much power must be a real head-rush*, Adam thought.

"Yes, yes I am," Kaylor stammered. In the brief time he'd had with Kaylor, Adam had never seen him this nervous.

The Juirean cocked his head slightly to the right. "Bring the two of them. I will require a room with no listening devices or images."

The Juirean then moved to Adam's cell. Adam did not stand, which seemed to irritate most of the Nimorians—and especially the Rigorians—who demanded that he stand before the Counselor. Adam just flashed a big, toothy grin at the lizards, which he knew would throw them into a crazed frenzy.

"SILENCE!" the Juirean commanded, and the Rigorians immediately ceased their chatter. Adam remained seated.

After scanning the pad, the Juirean turned to his right and began to leave the room. "Bring him, too," the Counselor commanded just before disappearing though the doorway.

The three prisoners were escorted to a large room in the same building featuring a wide desk set near the middle. Chairs were brought in for the Kaylor, Jym and Adam, while the Juirean slipped into a massive chair positioned behind the desk. He then signaled for everyone except the four of them to leave the room. Adam didn't question the Juirean's confidence in being left alone with the prisoners. After all, who would dare accost a Juirean? Adam continued to size up the Counselor as he took a seat.

Kaylor and Jym looked as though they'd pissed their pants. They sat hunched over slightly, occasionally daring a glance up at the Juirean. Then without ceremony, the Counselor began speaking:

"There will be no salvage of this craft," the Juirean stated bluntly. This got Kaylor and Jym's attention. "The ship is being confiscated by the Juirean Authority, and all records of its discovery have been purged from the Library."

"Forgive me, Counselor," Kaylor said feebly, "but that is a legitimate claim. Why can we not receive a salvage, or at least a recovery fee, for our efforts?"

"That ship is of unknown origin and therefore is to be taken to Melfora Lum at the demand of Overlord Oplim Ra Unis. You will provide all data regarding the location of the find, the direction from which the ship appeared, the circumstances of the recovery, as well as any observances once you entered the vessel."

Kaylor appeared crestfallen. Adam knew he had placed so much promise on the salvage, and now it was being ripped away from him. But Kaylor did not offer any resistance to the request—order—and began reciting exactly what had occurred over the past two days.

Damn! Has it only been two days since all this started? The thought suddenly made Adam grow very tired.

While Kaylor droned on, Adam noticed that the Juirean kept looking over at him. Their eyes would lock, and then the Counselor would casually return his attention to Kaylor. Once Kaylor had finished his deposition, the Juirean turned his full attention upon Adam.

"What were you doing aboard the ship?"

"I don't have any idea. Like I've been telling everyone, I was kidnapped—abducted. I woke up in one of those pods not knowing how I got there or why."

The Juirean just stared at him for several seconds. Then finally he asked, "You did not met any of the ship's crew or owners, or had any conversation with them?"

"The only living creature I saw was one of those gray things, but I couldn't understand anything it was saying, besides Kaylor, of course."

"And where are you from?"

"I'm from the planet Earth." Adam waited for the expected comment about dirt and such, but it never came.

The Counselor spoke: "Why would the owners of the ship be transporting your kind aboard? Does your planet have relationships with them?"

"No, I don't think so. We haven't had any confirmed contact with aliens—with other races—even though there have been a lot of stories."

"I guess the stories are true, now aren't they?" stated the Juirean, with an edge of sarcasm in his tone.

"I suppose so." Adam was getting tired of all this. "Listen, I just want to get back home. I'm not interested in any of this bullshit or any of your politics. I didn't ask to be here, and I could care less about whose ship that is and where it came from. We are not a star traveling species—"

"Then why were eighty of your species be onboard that ship? What value are you to its builders?"

"You haven't been listening to me, pal. I ... don't ... know."

Adam saw the veins in the Juirean's neck begin to twitch. He was sure the Juirean had never been spoken to like this before, but he didn't give a damn. This obnoxious blowhard was just another flamboyant bureaucrat on some kind of power trip.

"It is decided," the Juirean announced suddenly. "You will be transported to Melfora Lum to be interrogated by the Overlord himself." He turned to Kaylor and Jym. "And the two of you will be subjected to a brain cleansing to erase all memory of your encounter with the derelict ship."

Adam was too pissed off to notice the look of utter shock that came over the faces of his companions. "But we've done nothing wrong!" Kaylor cried out. "We promise we will not say anything about this."

"I will guarantee that you will not." The Counselor pressed a button on the desk, and about a dozen armed guards entered the room. "Take them back to their cells and arrange a link with the Overlord." The Juirean stood, glaring at Adam as he was removed from the room. Adam just sent him a wink.

A few minutes later, in another room in the Ministry, Fredic Dess listened in on the conversation the Counselor was having with his Overlord, as he reported on the results of the brief interrogation.

KLIN! Could this be true?

Whether it was or not, this information would make him rich. Angar had promised to pay him handsomely for any information he could provide regarding the prisoners. He had already given him their location within the Compound, as well as instructions on how to the best affect a rescue.

And now this.

He fingered the communication device and Angar answered immediately....

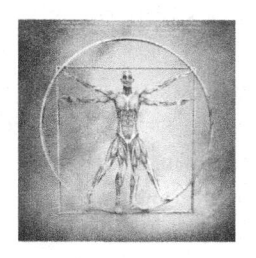

Chapter 16

The moment the cell door was closed and locked, Adam was already planning his escape. He was desperate now, determined to avoid accompanying the yellow-hair Juirean to yet another alien planet and more banal questioning about something he knew nothing about. But he would need Kaylor and Jym's help to get away; he just didn't have any idea how much help they would be.

Kaylor had fallen back on one of the cots in his cell and was just lying there, staring at the ceiling. Jym was on the other cot, but he balled up in the fetal position, giving off soft whimpering sounds. They both looked like lost causes to Adam.

Adam moved to the bars separating the two cells. "Listen up," he hissed. "We've gotta get out of here. There's no way I'm going to let them take me away with that asshole."

Kaylor continued to stare at the ceiling.

"Snap out of it! I need the two of you to pay attention."

"It's no use, Adam," Kaylor finally acknowledged. "There's nothing we can do at this point."

"Bullshit! What was he talking about in there, about some sort of a cleansing?"

Kaylor looked over at him. "A brain cleansing; they're going to erase our memories. They're supposed to be able to be selective, but I've never heard of a perfect cleansing. We are probably going to lose a couple years of memories, if not more. And then beings who have had it done are never the same."

"Then we have to get out of here while we have a chance."

Kaylor looked at him as if he was crazy. "Do you not see where we are?"

"I can get us out of here. But then we're going to have to get off this planet, and that's where you come in."

Kaylor sat up and Jym stopped his whimpering. "How—how can you get us out of here?"

Rather than tell them, Adam moved to the front of his cell, braced his back against the left side bars, and pushed against a front bar with his right leg. After a few grunts, the bar began to move. He then shifted sides and pushed on another bar until he had a separation wide enough to squeeze through.

Jym and Kaylor were standing at the bars of their cell, staring in shocked disbelief. "What *are* you?" Jym asked.

"Never mind," Adam said as he moved over to the bars between the two cells. Bracing himself against the cell wall as he had done earlier, he bent the bars wide enough for the two aliens to slip through and into his cell.

Soon they were all outside of the cages and in the corridor. To their left was the processing room, so they hurried off to the right. None of them had any idea what lie beyond the door at the end of the cell block, but Adam was willing to take his chances. The only plan he had at this time was to get back to Kaylor's ship and get the hell off of this god-forsaken planet. With so few options to choose from, action seemed like his best one.

They stopped at the door and Adam tested the handle. It was unlocked. He opened it a crack, just enough to see two Nimorians sitting at a desk, one gnawing on some food, the other typing on a keyboard.

Taking a deep breath, Adam burst through the door, and before the two creatures could react, Adam was upon them. He caught the typist with a right cross and felt his fist sink deep into the alien's skull with a splatter of blood and the cracking of bone. *Jesus Christ! I just ripped off half of his face!*

Adam then brought his left elbow across his body, striking the other Nimorian on the back of the head. Again the cracking of bone, and soon both aliens lay on the floor, dead. With his right hand covered in alien blood and brain matter, Adam quickly removed the sidearms from the guards and strapped one around his waist. He tossed the other holster to Kaylor, who promptly had it fall through his hands and onto the floor.

"Pick it up, damn it. Put it on."

Kaylor bent over and obeyed, his mouth hanging open as he surveyed the carnage Adam had just caused. Adam just shrugged it off. Casualties of war....

Quickly taking in their surroundings, Adam found that they were in a foyer, with a flight of stairs leading up and another long, deserted hallway leading away from the desk. At the far end of the hallway was a set of double glass doors with what looked like a large room beyond and natural light streaming in. With an MK-17 in hand, Adam hurried down the hall toward the exit with Kaylor and Jym close behind.

Almost immediately, three Nimorians appeared out of a side room, nearly colliding with them. As the aliens panicked and went for their weapons, Adam calmly placed three quick bolts of blue fire into them as he sped past, hardly breaking stride. In this case, the weapon's targeting computer never did vibrate, as it found nothing to lock on to. *What a worthless piece of shit,* Adam thought.

Suddenly, a violent explosion rocked the entire building. The double doors at the end of the hallway shattered inward and clouds of black smoke billowed into the hall toward the trio. Screams and yelling could be heard all around, interlaced with electric popping sounds.

Cut off from his original exit point, Adam crashed through a door on his right trailing Kaylor and Jym behind him. They were in a large stock room, occupied by a panicked Nimorian, who alerted by the explosion, was running toward the same door. Adam lowered his shoulder and crashed into the alien, sending him flying backwards, impacting a stack of crates before falling limp to the floor.

The room was lined with metal shelving easily thirty feet high and stacked with boxes and other equipment. Filling the interior floor space were several multi-level rows of stacked crates. Adam spotted a second door at the far end of the room, and the three of them set off for it.

There were more explosions along with deeper sounds of electric popping. The whole building was under siege.

Just then, three more Nimorians, along with a trio of Rigorians, burst through the far door. Spotting the escapees—and not knowing whether they were friend or foe—the aliens brought their weapons to firing positions.

Adam chose to get off the first shots, but before he could, the six guards opened up with their more-powerful flash rifles, filling the air with reckless bolts in Adam's direction. He dove behind a stack of crates just as the first electric balls whizzed past. The shots were high and wide, but they continued to come in rapid succession.

Kaylor and Jym piled on top of him as they, too, dove for cover. Adam shoved them off and crawled to the edge of the crate he was behind. A quick glance verified that the guards were spreading out, moving toward them. He spotted one of the lizards about thirty feet away, in plain sight. He let loose with a bolt, striking the Rigorian in the gut. Another came right behind him, and Adam fired again. This time he missed to the right, and when he corrected his aim and depressed the trigger, nothing happened.

"Your charge is dry!" Kaylor yelled. Adam twisted a lever on the handle of MK, dropping the spent charge pack to the floor. Then pulling another from the holster belt, he snapped it in. There no more packs on his belt, so he reached over and pulled two from Kaylor's belt. He wouldn't be needing them anyway.

Performing a quick recon, Adam saw that a stacked row of crates to his right would provide a path on its second level, shielded from the view of the aliens.

"Stay here," he said to Kaylor and Jym, then he slid off to his right, and in a single bound in the light gravity, jumped to the top of the first layer of crates, about six feet high. Moving quickly along this level, hidden by the upper layer of crates, Adam managed to get behind the two remaining Rigorians. Grimacing at the reckless act he was about to commit, Adam vaulted into the air and landed on the floor about ten feet behind the two aliens. As they turned, Adam let off two precise shots, killing them both instantly.

The lizards carried long-barrel rifles of some kind, so Adam snatched one up—and dropped for cover just as the three Nimorians opened up on his position.

Adam found a thick piece of packing wood on the floor near him, broken free of a nearby crate by one of the bolts. Testing its weight, he tossed the piece of wood high and to his right. As it landed, the three Nimorians shifted their fire toward the sound. Adam stood—rifle stock pressed securely into his right shoulder—and found he was looking straight down a line of aliens, all in a row, looking to his right. Taking aim at the first one in line, he fingered the trigger.

A bright bolt of electric blue light shot from the barrel, striking the first alien along the front of his chest; the bolt then continued to the second alien, impacting his neck. Both went down. *Two with one shot, not bad.* Then as the third alien turned to watch his two companions collapse to the floor, the last thing he ever saw was an ever-growing bolt of blue energy, heading straight for his face.

After the kill, Adam darted between crates and back to where he'd left Kaylor and Jym. As he rounded the box and slid in beside them, Jym let out a high-pitched cry, and Kaylor's eyes rolled back in his head, nearly fainting.

"Don't surprise us like that!" Kaylor scolded.

"Let's go." Adam commanded, ignoring him. But just as they stood, five more Nimorians entered the room through the far door.

As new barrage of blue bolts came zipping their way, they dove back for cover again behind the crate. Now desperate for an alternative exit, Adam noticed a break in the metal shelving units lining the wall. He had an idea.

"Follow me, and stay low."

Adam took off, with the other two close behind. They reached the break in the shelving and crowded in for cover, with splashes of blue bolts dancing around them. With his back against the wall, Adam struck the surface with his left elbow and was relieved to feel the wallboard break. He had been hoping that this was an interior wall; the outer walls of the building were made of brick and he wasn't sure he could break through those. But these thin, inner walls were a breeze. He smashed his elbow into the wall several more times until he had opened up a three-foot wide gap. Then pressing his full weight against it, Adam crashed through the wall and into another room, landing on his back with his legs still in the hole, rifle across his chest.

To his shock, two Nimorians had just sped past his position, heading for the battle at the other end of the building, weapons ready. Seeing Adam, they turned and took aim. Rolling to his right, Adam fired the rifle, striking one of the aliens in the chest. Then just as he let loose with another bolt at the second alien, a bolt of energy erupted from the Nimorian's weapon. Rolling on his back, the bolt ripped across the front of Adam's tunic, burning through it, exposing his chest and the angry red burn from where Kaylor had shot him two days before. His own shot found its mark, striking the guard in the forehead.

Adam quickly regained his feet, breathing a sigh of relief that he was still alive. Then reaching through the opening in the wall, he yanked both Kaylor and Jym through, and they all ended up standing in the middle of the corridor, coughing and covered with white dust and bits of wallboard.

Adam surveyed the hallway quickly. There were several large windows set in the opposite wall, dim yellow light shining through. Adam crossed to the nearest one and smashed out the glass with the butt of the rifle. The window was big enough to crawl through, so Adam shoved Jym and Kaylor through the opening, before following.

Once outside, Adam pressed against the warm brick wall, and with his left arm forced Jym and Kaylor to do the same. They were in the space between two of the Ministry buildings, separated by about sixty feet. To their left a battle was raging, with two groups squared off against each other, firing from inside doorways and behind vehicles.

The three of them were fully exposed, with dozens of windows from both buildings facing the grassy area. Luckily, the sun was beginning to set, casting deep shadows in the space between the buildings. The blue tunics both he and Kaylor wore, along with Jym's dark green one, would help provide some camouflage. To his right, and about a hundred feet away, was the wall surrounding the Ministry Compound.

"Stay low and close to the building," Adam whispered, as he set off for the wall, hugging the side of the building as they went. If anyone in the buildings noticed their movement, they chose to ignore them in light of the intense fighting taking place at the other end of the building. They made it to the wall without incident.

Pressing his back against the barricade, Adam surveyed each direction for any guard towers set the wall. Seeing none, he stood and grabbed Jym by his tunic. "Trust me," he said, and promptly tossed the much smaller creature up to the top of the twelve-foot high wall. Jym clung there, with an arm and a leg dangling precariously over each side. Kaylor was more cooperative, and allowed himself to be hurled onto the wall as well. Adam then tossed the bolt rifle over to the other side.

With an easy leap in the light gravity, Adam was able to reach the top of the wall with both hands and propel himself over in one fluid motion. He landed softly on the ground beyond, and then called for Jym and Kaylor, one at a time, to drop into his arms.

They were in a greenbelt area about ninety feet wide between the wall and a road that ran parallel to the Ministry Compound. Beyond the road were several streets heading away from the

Compound and lined with buildings of various heights. A short distance to their left was the nearest street intersection, where several creatures had gathered, looking in the direction of the Ministry, curious at all the explosions and gunfire taking place there. In the gray light of dusk, none had noticed the three escapees scale the wall, so Adam picked up the rifle and led them in a sprint for the cover of the nearest building.

Crouching against the building, Adam noticed both Jym and Kaylor panting heavily, trying to catch their breath. *Out of shape aliens,* Adam observed. *Go figure!*

Inside the Compound, the sounds of the battle could still be heard, but they were growing less intense. Adam pulled Kaylor near. "Which way to the spaceport?"

Kaylor pointed to their right. "This way," he panted. "It's about twenty minutes away by foot. Maybe we should find a transport for hire?"

"You want us to call a cab?" Adam shot back. "I've got a better idea."

On the nearby street were several of the native wheeled transports, looking like small SUV's from back home. Creatures of various shapes and sizes were milling around, chattering and pointing toward the Compound and the rising column of black smoke, easily visible in the late afternoon sky.

At one of the cars, its occupant had climbed out and was standing at the open door, looking toward the Compound. Adam moved up behind him, dropped the rifle, and then used both his hands to grab the alien by the back of his shirt and the seat of his pants. He tossed him high into the air, and the creature landed hard about ten feet away in a patch of bushes at the side of the street.

"Get in!" Adam yelled, as he slipped into the driver's seat.

Of course, Adam had never driven an alien car before, but he had observed how it was done during the drive to the Compound earlier that morning. In the center console was a joystick with a flat handle on top, and once Jym had climbed in the back and Kaylor into the front passenger seat, Adam pushed the stick all the way forward with purpose.

But nothing happened. He pushed again ... still nothing. Then Kaylor calmly reached over and flicked a switch on the dashboard.

The vehicle lunged forward, sideswiping another car before Adam could throttle back and steer the car back into the center of the road. He quickly got the feel of the controls, and soon they were racing down the road and toward the spaceport.

Most of the traffic on the road was heading in the opposite direction, toward the Ministry Compound, so they made it back to the spaceport in less than five minutes.

Barreling through the main gate, Adam was half expecting to see a contingent of Ministry police waiting for them; they couldn't outrun radios or telephones, or whatever they used on this planet. But there was no one there, not even the incredibly bloated alien at the guard hut. However, there were other creatures in the spaceport, but most of them were scurrying about, apparently readying their craft for liftoff, and paid no special attention to Adam's speeding vehicle.

News of the raid on the Ministry Compound had spread fast, and even though no one knew exactly what was going on, very few creatures in the spaceport were willing to wait around and find out. Like true mariners everywhere, whether at sea or in space, they preferred their chances off-land, rather than as sitting ducks stuck in port.

Adam pulled back on the joystick and the car skidded to a halt at the base of the ramp leading up to the cargo hold of the *FS-475*. Kaylor jumped out and ran to a panel cover set in the skin of the ship. Flipping it open, he punched in a code and the door to the cargo bay opened. The three of them ran up the protruding ramp and into the ship.

As Jym secured the door and retracted the ramp, Kaylor and Adam hurried to the pilothouse. Jym was only steps behind.

"How long until we can take off?" Adam yelled as he fastened his safety harness.

Both Kaylor and Jym were frantically pushing buttons and pulling levers. "When on-planet, I always keep one of the main generators humming, just in case we have to bolt out fast," Kaylor cried out. "Even then, it's still going to take about five minutes before we've built up enough compression to pull us up."

Adam didn't have any idea what Kaylor was talking about, but he sounded convincing. So for the next few minutes, as the two aliens went about their pre-flight chores, Adam nervously peered through the open viewport and across the ever-darkening spaceport, expecting at any moment to see streaks from electric balls of energy, or the deafening blast of an explosion.

Instead, there came the sickening feeling of vertigo as the ship's gravity well engaged and overrode that of the planet's own attraction. Then, without any sense of movement on their part, it was as if the whole spaceport moved away from them at incredible speed. And then the entire city fell away, followed quickly by the surrounding land, and finally the planet itself.

They were back in space, and to his surprise, Adam began to relax.

But not so Kaylor and Jym. Adam could see the look of worry on their faces. As the spherical shape of the planet became more pronounced, and the bright layer of atmosphere grew thinner, the two of them were staring intently at their view screens.

"Is everything okay?' Adam finally asked.

"It looks like two other craft have slipped in behind us," Jym answered.

"From the surface—"

"No," Jym interrupted. "They were already in orbit."

"What are you going to do?"

Kaylor leaned back in his seat. "Nothing right now," he said. "They're not closing on us, just lying back, following."

"So where do we go now?" Adam asked.

"Maybe you should have thought of that before you broke us out of the Ministry!" Jym barked out. "I don't have any idea where we can go—"

"I have a suggestion."

The voice came from behind them, from the door to the pilothouse.

In unison, the three of them jerked their heads around, only to find a tall, dark figure standing in the doorway, bolt weapon aimed at them. Three other creatures stood behind him in the hallway, each with their own weapon pointed into the room.

Leaning into the pilothouse, the speaker handed Jym a piece of paper.

"What is that?" Kaylor asked Jym.

Jym looked up from the paper at Kaylor. "It's the coordinates of the Kyllian Asteroids."

Adam didn't hear any of the exchange, nor did he notice the look of shock on Kaylor's face at the mention of the Kyllian Asteroids. Instead he sat in stunned silence as he stared at the creature in the doorway.

It was another Human—and he was staring directly into Adam's eyes!

Chapter 17

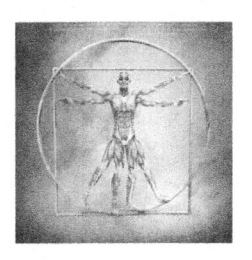

"You must be Adam Cain," the Human said. He stepped further into the room, until he was about six feet from Adam. "And I am Riyad Tarazi."

Adam was speechless. Mouth agape, he did and said nothing as Riyad's men swept into the room and disarmed them. Riyad then turned to Jym. "Enter in those coordinates, and then let's all go up to the common room for a little chat."

The man, Riyad Tarazi, was right at six-feet tall, heavily muscled, with tight, jet black hair on his head and beard. His eyes were dark, as was his complexion, and the accent was unmistakable. As Riyad's men escorted the trio to the common room, Adam had no doubt: Tarazi was either Arab or Iranian. He also found it strange, that at a time when he should have felt overwhelming excitement at finding another of his kind, all Adam could see before him was a threat. And, remarkably, it was a greater threat than anything else he'd encountered to date in this strange, new universe....

Jym and Kaylor sat on the couch as Riyad took a seat at the table. Adam chose to stand. "Come, sit my brother," Riyad said, offering a seat at the table, as the three other creatures—of a species Adam had not seen before—fanned out around the room, maintaining their guard with weapons ready.

Reluctantly, Adam sat down.

Leaning forward, Riyad reached out and grabbed Adam's arm. "I am so pleased to see you, Mr. Cain," he said sincerely, with a large, bright smile. "I was wondering if I would *ever* see another Human again. We will talk again at length, but later."

Then releasing Adam, Riyad turned his attention to Kaylor. "But first things first. You," he said directly to Kaylor, "You have something of mine, and I want it back."

Kaylor tried to look more upset than scared. He sat on the edge of the couch and said, "Who are *you* to come aboard my ship with weapons upon us? I do not know you, and I'm sure I have nothing that belongs to you."

Riyad just smiled. "Oh, yes you do. You took it from me a few days ago after my men had spent considerable time and effort to secure it." Kaylor had suspected, but now he knew for sure; his heart began to race. "And then to make matters worse, you managed to abscond with the *one* thing aboard that had more value to me than all the other riches within that alien ship—*the computer core.*"

What did he just say? Adam turned to Kaylor. "*You* have the computer core? Why didn't you tell me! That thing can help me get home."

"That's exactly right, my Human brother," said Riyad. "That one item is more important to the two of us then they can possibly imagine. So he didn't tell you he hid the core somewhere in the asteroids?"

"No, no he didn't," Adam said between gritted teeth. "Why the hell not?"

"I couldn't tell you because we were not supposed to have it," Kaylor pleaded in his defense. "We are not allowed to take anything from a derelict until the salvage is awarded."

"So why *did* you take it?"

"Because, as I told you, it can take months for the salvage process to go through, and then there can be counter-claims and disputes. I wanted to make sure we'd get something for risking our lives—"

"And so you chased off my captains and took *my* prize," Riyad said as he rose from his chair and walked the short distance over to Kaylor.

Then in a move almost too swift to see, Riyad grabbed Kaylor by his tunic, lifted him, and pinned him against the bulkhead, his feet dangling easily a foot off the floor. "And now with your lie, the damn Juireans think *we* took the core! And they will not rest until they get it."

Riyad released him, letting Kaylor fall unceremoniously to the floor. Then he walked casually over to the food counter, pressed a few buttons, and returned to the table with two drinks in hand. He sat down, placing one of the drinks in front of Adam. Kaylor sheepishly returned to the couch.

After taking a long gulp of his drink, Riyad leaned back in the chair and propped his booted feet up on the table. "Neither one of you have any idea as to the significance of that ship, do you?" he said to Kaylor and Jym. "Let me tell you." He took another long swig off his drink. "The ship you so brazenly took from my men was a *Klin* starship."

The two aliens—and even Adam—were shocked by the revelation.

"*Klin!* Are you sure?" Jym had found his voice.

"Positive. Now you can understand why the Juireans have interceded, and why your lies have put me, and my men, in such a dangerous predicament?"

He waited for a moment to let the full impact of his disclosure sink in, and then he gave a subtle nod to his guards. Two of them descended on Kaylor and Jym, holding them down on the couch as they locked ankle bracelets on each of them. It only took a few seconds, and then the guards resumed their posts.

"What are you doing?" Kaylor yelled, grabbing at the foreign object on his leg.

"Each of those bracelets contain a small explosive charge," Riyad said. "It should be small enough not to cause any widespread damage to your ship, but definitely strong enough to blow off both your legs—and undoubtedly bring about your deaths. I have taken this action to guarantee that you will cooperate with my demands." He took another gulp of his drink. "Now ... you will recover the stolen computer core and hand it over to me. If you do this without any resistance, I will release you and send you on your way. If not ...." He pulled a small black box out of his pocket, "all I have to do is press in a code here, and you will not live to see another day."

Riyad seemed to revel in watching the look of horror on the faces of the two aliens. Then after finishing off his drink, he asked, "Do I make myself clear?" They both nodded emphatically.

"You don't have to do this," Kaylor said. "The computer core has caused me enough problems. I just want to get it out of my life."

"Good," said Riyad. "Then we have an understanding. I just want to make sure I have your full cooperation for the duration of our time together."

Adam was equally shocked at the drastic action Riyad had taken. He wanted the information from the core as well, but this was kind of harsh. Kaylor looked at him. "Adam isn't there anything you can do to help us? I did save your life on that ship...."

Adam felt numb inside as he heard Kaylor beg. Then he turned to face Kaylor. "You lied to me, Kaylor. I didn't want to take the core from you. I just wanted to learn the location of Earth from it. After that, it was all yours. And as far as saving my life, I believe I just saved the two of you from having your memories scraped clean. I think we'll call it even."

Even as he spoke, Adam couldn't believe the words that were coming from his mouth. He never considered himself a particularly cruel person, but right now he was seething with anger. For the past few days, he had been on a roller-coaster ride of emotions, one moment feeling like he had a chance to get home and back to Maria and Cassie, then the next having his hopes crushed underfoot. And Kaylor had the core all along.

"Just get the core and everything should be okay—"

Just then, Adam felt something grab his ankle, and when he sprung out of the chair and looked around, he saw Riyad bent over under the table. Adam backed away and looked down at his ankle. He now had a bracelet fastened on his ankle, too. "What the fuck!" he yelled at Riyad. The guards moved in, weapons pointed at Adam.

Riyad calmly leaned back in the chair, looking incredibly satisfied with himself. "Sorry, my friend, but you are an extremely dangerous creature. I cannot take the chance that you will not attack me or my men. This is for your own good."

"*My own good!* How do you figure?" He placed his foot on the chair and began to examine the device. It was a simple black metal band with a small box about the size of a cigarette pack welded on it. There didn't seem to be any access to the box from what he could see or latch on the band.

"Mr. Cain, we both need the core, and we both want to get home. I may have to do some pretty nasty things to get the cooperation I need, and I don't want you to start growing a conscience. Besides, you are a Human; I could certainly use you in a fight. I just want to make sure you're going to be on my side, if and when the time comes."

Adam was a trained SEAL, an underwater demolition expert. He knew explosive devices and had a fair knowledge of how to disarm them. But now was not the time to reveal this information. After all, he certainly would not be allowed to disarm the device—

even if it was possible—not in a room full of armed guards. There should come a time when he would be alone, when he could take a closer look at the device....

What he had to do now was put this Riyad Tarazi character at ease. The pirate definitely thought he had the upper hand, and considering that the ankle bomb was made from some alien technology of which Adam knew nothing of, there was a pretty good chance he was right.

Calmly, Adam sat back down. "Listen *Riyad*, I don't want to be any trouble," Adam said softly. "I just want to get home, just like you. Promise me that once you get the core, that you'll keep your word about taking off these things."

"As one Human to another, you have my word."

Regrettably, the statement didn't make Adam feel any better....

Chapter 18

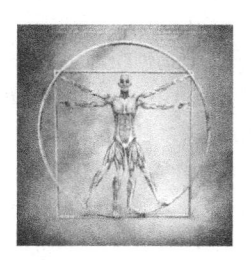

Feeling as if he no longer had to keep all the players under guard, Riyad allowed everyone to clean up, go to the restroom if they needed, and to get something to eat. They would be at the asteroid belt in about five hours, so he had Adam show him to his room, where they could have a more private conversation.

As they entered, the first thing Riyad did was crank up the gravity to a more respectable level. He said to Adam, "I rarely leave my ship because of the gravity issue. K'ly, the planet where my pirate base is located, is a little more than three-quarters Earth's gravity. If I spent too much time there, I'd grow weak and lose my edge."

Adam sat backwards in the chair, resting his arms on the back and facing the bed, which Riyad had claimed. The pirate leader propped pillows against the bulkhead and leaned back, stretching his legs out in front of him and locking his hands behind his head.

"There, now we are both comfortable. Let's catch up." He flashed Adam a wide grin. "So where are you from, Mr. Cain? You're American, aren't you?"

"That's right. And you're Middle Eastern."

"Lebanese originally, but I spent most of my adult life in Pakistan, and even some time in your country. So please tell me, Adam, what year and day is it on Earth?"

Adam was surprised by the question. "I'm not quite sure. I don't have any idea how long I was asleep on the … on the Klin ship. But the last day I remember was October 23rd, 2011."

"Ah ha!" Riyad exclaimed. "I was so close. I had no way of knowing time, so at one point, years ago, I counted one-thousand-one, one-thousand-two and so forth until I estimated a minute. And then set a device to count off the intervals. I figured it was around

2011, but I'm off by about four months by my calculations. Not bad for an estimate, wouldn't you say?"

"So how long have you be out … here? And how did you end up being the leader of the pirates?" This was actually something Adam was anxious to learn.

"I've been here for about six years, and I'm sure my story is very similar to yours. One day was in the mountains near the Afghan-Pakistani border when I remember seeing a bright light—and then nothing. I woke up to find I was aboard a spaceship of some kind—but certainly without the fancy accommodations you had on the *Klin* ship." He smiled broadly again. "I was in a cell—a cage really—with three other Humans and several other creatures. The conditions were horrible; we slept on straw pads and drank filthy water. The food we were given was alien and without the computer testing like you have here. We were all sick with food poisoning for several days. Two of my fellow Humans died during the trip.

"Then we were transferred to another ship—sold, I believe—to a group of pirates. After about a week—I think it was about a week—we landed on a planet and were taken out to be sold again. Not taking too kindly to the idea of being a slave, I fought back and started a mini riot on the auction block. My one remaining Human companion, a gentleman name Ashbar from India, was killed in the riot.

"But I survived, and instead caught the attention of one of the pirate captains, who offered me a place in his crew. He was impressed with my fighting skills," Riyad said with a wicked smile.

He stopped his story and narrowed his eyes. "You must know by now, my friend, that we Humans have certain advantages over most of the other creatures out here. In fact, I understand you defeated two Rigorians during a duel your first day on Nimor. That is no easy task."

"I didn't pick that fight! *They* challenged me," Adam said in his defense.

"Oh, I'm not being critical. I'm just pointing out a fact. In the six years I have been out here, I have found creatures who were faster, who were stronger and who were tougher than we are. Some even exhibited remarkable intelligence and coordination. But *none* combine all these traits into one being like we do. Out here, *we are the supermen*. No, we can't fly, and we can certainly be killed by the weapons they possess, but none of the creatures I've encountered can stand against us in a fair fight."

"What about the Juireans?"

Riyad pursed his lips. "I've never met a Juirean before, but from what I've heard, they may be a challenge. But I had also heard how tough the Rigorians were, and both of us have made easy work of them. But I have to admit, I have been trained at combat and considered an accomplished warrior where I come from."

Adam tensed. His one advantage over his fellow Human was the fact that he didn't know Adam's profession or skill-set. In fact, as he listened, Adam was beginning to believe Riyad might have been a terrorist in his past life.

"You were in the military?" Adam asked, trying to pull more details out of the conversation.

Riyad just laughed. "I guess you could say that. As an American, I'm not sure I should be telling you this, but for a while I was a face in a deck of cards that your military carried with them in Iraq."

Adam couldn't play ignorant any longer. "You were a *terrorist!*" Adam tried to display as much shock and outrage as possible.

"I was a *freedom fighter*," Riyad corrected without a trace of indignation. "My cause was just, and I have no regrets fighting the infidels who invaded our lands and killed our women and children," he continued, his voice nearly musical in nature. Adam got the sense Riyad was reciting a standard line. It all seemed so strange.

"Why do I sense that you don't really believe that anymore?" Adam asked.

"Well ... look around you, my friend." Riyad said, with a sweeping motion of his hand. "You can't tell me that your belief in the Christian god has not been shaken over the past few days? It's hard to maintain your faith in light of the reality we both find ourselves in."

"You mean all this alien life in the galaxy? I was never that strong of a believer myself," Adam offered.

"Oh, don't be mistaken, neither was I. That's why I was *leader* in the movement, and not just one of the foot soldiers. Suicide bombers are reserved for the young and most-devout of our faith. The only time you'd see one the senior commanders take his own life—to meet Allah and our seventy-two virgins—was when he had no choice."

"By the way ... we got Osama," Adam interjected, just to pick the scab.

"Captured?"

"No, killed. And in his pajamas."

"That's a shame," was all Riyad said, with little emotion. "But he was more of a figurehead than our true leader. You do know he was not the one who planned the attack on your country? He was just the money man, and helped supply some of the manpower for the attack."

"Oh, we got Khalid Sheik Mohamed, too."

Riyad just shrugged. "We all knew the risks we were taking. But that is all in the past now, my friend. We have both been shown a new future for our planet, as well as our race."

"What do you mean?"

The pirate leaned over onto one elbow. "Mr. Cain, the Klin have plans for the Human race; why else would they be transporting eighty of our kind through hostile territory unless we are important to them. The Juireans have now learned that the Klin still exist, and they certainly will not let the Earth remain unharmed knowing that the Klin find us of value."

"What do the Klin want with *us*?"

"My guess is they are aware of our abilities. There is no telling how many of their ships have made it to and from Earth over the years, bringing Humans to some unknown destination." Then he grew very serious. "I believe the Klin are building a *Human* army."

Adam was shocked by this revelation, but he couldn't dispute it. "Why, so we can fight against the Juireans?"

"That would be my guess." Riyad laughed and leaned back on the pillows. "And they couldn't have picked a better race for the task. We *are* pretty proficient killers; just look what we do to our own kind. Imagine what we could do against an alien enemy."

Adam shook his head. "You come from a culture, one that doesn't value life as much as we do," Adam countered. "I don't think we're as blood-thirsty as you believe."

"Bullshit, Mr. Cain! You've only been out here for a few days ... and how many of these aliens have you already killed?"

"This isn't a god-damn video game! We're not keeping score."

"Sure we are," Riyad shot back. "It's us against them. That's just the way of the world. When we Humans are faced with an enemy, we put aside all our *humanity* and treat that enemy as essentially as *non*-Human, just objects to the eliminated. I can prove it to you. Take a normal person, let's say someone who works in a convenience store, who then joins the military and is sent out to kill other people—other Humans. When he comes back home, to the so-called real-world, no one—not even he—considers himself to be a murderer. He is celebrated, and can sleep peacefully at night, content in the knowledge that his killing was justified.

"Now let that same man walk into a bank and shoot the teller. Now he is the most-vile of creatures, to be scorned and ridiculed, the basest of our kind.

"You see, when you kill in war, it's different. That's why you Westerners keep calling us animals and savages, because you think we are killing indiscriminately. We are not. We are at war, and that makes all the difference. At least it does for us. And if we treat our own kind—Human kind—in such a manner, then killing aliens ... well, we wouldn't give *that* a second thought, and we'd feel no shame in doing so."

"I thought you said all of that was in your past—*my friend*," Adam said sarcastically.

"Old habits die hard."

Adam knew he had a point. As a Navy SEAL, Adam had never concerned himself too much with the enemy he'd killed in combat. In fact, he never gave it a second thought. Granted, he had seen horrific things on the battlefield, and that had upset him to a degree. The burned and maimed bodies, the bloody, ripped apart corpses, the vacant, hollow eyes of the dead—*that* you had trouble getting used to. But score one for the good guys, is how he always justified it. It was them or us—just as Riyad had said. And he also had to admit, that when he had killed the Rigorian lizards, as well as the Nimorians guards in the security building, he hadn't felt a trace of remorse in doing so. It had been like stepping on a bug....

Riyad was studying Adam's face as he went through his mental exercise, a sly smile on the terrorist's face. "You know I'm right," he stated. "We would be the perfect warriors for the Klin."

Adam shook his head. "This is not our war. I'm really sorry that the Klin were screwed over by the Juireans thousands of years ago—talk about holding grudges—but we have no motivation to fight the Juireans."

"Not yet. But once the Juireans learn of our importance to the Klin, they will come down on us with everything they have. And then we *will* fight."

Damn it! This asshole keeps coming up with good points, Adam thought. "So what can we do about it?"

"For starters, we can keep the computer core out of the hands of the Juireans." Riyad sat up and moved to the edge of the bed. He was suddenly very animated. "We have a great opportunity here, to bring to our homeworld the gift of the universe." Riyad's eyes grew wide, even wild-looking. "Imagine what a power we could become with the technology of the Juireans, of star travel and of energy weapons. With our skills of war, we could direct our talents toward other enemies, and not toward our fellow Humans. We've never been able to do that before; we've never had an enemy outside of ourselves. In the end, *Humans* would be the new force in the galaxy!"

This line of thinking seemed very familiar. In fact, it was what Kaylor had told him about the early Juireans, the ones who had built The Mass, to help redirect their own primitive, warlike nature toward outside enemies, real or perceived. And Riyad was saying that Humanity should follow the same path as the Juireans.

Adam studied the terrorist as he spoke; he had an almost insane look on his face while describing his vision for how Humans would enter the community of civilizations in the galaxy. Is this how Adam would have imagined it? He had never put much thought into it, having never been that big of a science fiction fan. Yet he hoped that Riyad's way would not be the only way, where Humans would be introduced to the galaxy as a savage horde of war-mongering beasts, spreading out among the stars like a plague. Of course, Adam may have been a little melodramatic in his assessment, but on the other hand, he also knew the dark side of his race. He wasn't sure if Humanity was ready for the universe. Not quite yet.

"Why do we have to go out as a force—as you call it—at all? Why not as friends, as partners with the other races in the galaxy?" Even as he spoke the words, he knew they sounded hollow.

Riyad just smiled back at him, almost a sympathy-smile for an innocent child. "I don't know what kind of life you had back in America, Mr. Cain, but I do not hold such a naïve view of our fellow man. I have seen incredible injustices done by man towards man—"

"Often in the name of religion, I might point out," said Adam angrily.

"No doubt, but that doesn't change the fact that we, as a species, have survived and spread across our planet by killing our own kind and taking their land and possessions. That *is* how we will spread across the galaxy as well. It is our nature. And now we have the opportunity to direct that natural aggressiveness against creatures other than Human."

Then it dawned on Adam. "With *you* as our leader, I suppose?"

Riyad stared back at him for a moment before answering. "Why not? Someone has to lead, and I have more experience with the aliens than anyone else."

Now it was all coming clear. This megalomaniac wanted to return to Earth as its ruler, using the advanced technology of the Juireans to make that a reality. And then he planned on leading mankind in a galactic war that would cost millions, if not billions of Human lives. It was one thing to defend oneself against an enemy; it was quite another to instigate a war just for one's own selfish ambitions. It may very well come down to Humans having to defend themselves against a Juirean threat, but the way Riyad made it sound, he wanted to *provoke* a war just so he could become the savior, the hero of any such conflict.

And then Adam suddenly laughed out loud, as the absurdity of the conversation struck him. Riyad recoiled slightly. "What's so funny," he asked, sounding insulted.

"Are you serious? Just look at us," Adam began. "We're two measly Humans, sitting in a room aboard a spaceship, thousands of light years from our home, and we're seriously talking about leading an entire planet in a galactic war against an alien empire spanning thousands of worlds. When did we enter the *Twilight Zone?* What the fuck! We probably won't even survive the next few days, let alone long enough to return to Earth and lead the entire planet on some holy crusade against an alien empire. You really have to be crazy to think like that."

Riyad stood suddenly, his jaw locked in anger. "You are wrong, Mr. Cain! Humans have a destiny that must be fulfilled, and the events of the next few days will determine whether or not we fulfill that destiny. I *will* get the core, and I *will* find the location of Earth. Then we'll see which one of us is crazy!"

Riyad then stormed out of the room, leaving Adam wide-eyed and a little stunned at his reaction. It was all so surreal. But then he figured it probably wasn't the first time in his life that Riyad Tarazi had been called crazy.

Chapter 19

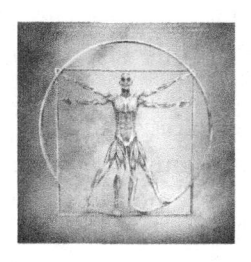

With Riyad gone, Adam had his first real opportunity to inspect the bomb strapped to his ankle. The band itself seemed to have melded together leaving no latch of any kind, and the box where the explosive was held was seamless as well, leaving no way to gain access to the interior. The only solution he could see would be to cut away the device from his ankle. But what could he use, and was the metal even capable of being cut? He tried bending it, and found the metal to be malleable. That would make it easier to get cutter between his ankle and the bomb. What he needed was something like a flexible pipe-cutter, a sort of serrated wire that he could use to file through the metal.

There might be something like that in the cargo hold, Adam thought. And with free-reign of the ship, he could go there now and see what he could find. But as the door to his stateroom slid open, he found himself face-to-face with Jym, the alien looking pale and nervous.

Startled, it took Jym a moment to collect himself, then he said, "We are nearing the asteroids, and the pirate wants you to come to the pilothouse right away." Jym seemed to be numb with fear. Besides everything else that had taken place over the past two days, Adam knew the bomb on Jym's ankle was freaking him out, as it would anyone.

Silently, Adam followed Jym back up to the pilothouse, which was packed with people. Riyad didn't acknowledge him as he entered, so Adam leaned against the far wall, next to the doorway.

The outer viewport shield was open and Adam could see out into the darkness of space. If there was an asteroid belt out there, it was impossible to tell. He couldn't see a single thing outside except for the blaze of stars off in the distance. There was no great cluster of floating rocks, looking like giant potatoes, all in close proximity of each other, like he'd seen in all the movies. As it had been with most things he'd experienced in this strange universe, he was mildly disappointed.

Riyad stood behind Kaylor, who was busy working the control stick of the ship. And then Adam saw something off in the distance. It looked like a dim flare that seemed to be growing brighter. Soon he could make out a small cylinder, which grew as the seconds passed. It was the pod, approaching them on chemical power.

Riyad looked back at Adam, no kindness in his gaze. "You have weak thoughts, Mr. Cain," he said to him. "You will always be a weak man."

Ouch. He's still pissed at being called crazy, Adam thought, smiling back at the pirate. *You just wait until I get this bomb off my ankle. Then you'll see just how weak I really am.*

Moments later Kaylor had brought the pod back into the ship, and by robotics, moved it into the cargo hold. They all adjourned to the larger room as Kaylor entered the pod and emerged a few moments later carrying the elusive computer core.

Adam was again disappointed. The almighty computer core that everyone was so enamored with was just a relatively plain looking metal box about three feet square. But even though it didn't look that impressive, Adam found himself growing ever more excited at the prospect of what information the box contained. In one form or another, it would reveal the location of the Earth; whether or not Adam could use that information to actually get home remained to be seen. But first things first....

Kaylor brought the box over to the workbench with the computer screen imbedded in the wall above and Jym stepped up to begin connecting cables to the device. Soon the lights on the face began to illuminate, and Riyad moved in closer. Everyone began to focus on the screen in the wall as Jym began to type feverishly on the keypad on the workbench.

Symbols began to appear on the screen. Adam couldn't read alien, so unless the information could be spoken and deciphered by the translation bug, he would never be able to understand the data. This he had not counted on.

Riyad seemed to be growing just as distraught as Adam. His eyes were wide and his jaw was set. He grabbed the back of Jym's tunic, "What is this crap?" he yelled at a sweating alien.

"I'm sorry," Jym pleaded, his voice shrill, "but it appears to be encrypted, or else there's a compatibility issue with our system."

"Don't fuck with me, you rodent!"

"No, no. I can't make it work! It needs to be hooked into a compatible module."

Riyad released Jym and began to pace the room, with all eyes upon him. Then he abruptly stopped and faced Kaylor, "Take us back to Nimor. We have to get aboard the Klin ship." Then he said to his guards, "Secure the core. No one is to get near it except me." He looked directly at Adam as he spoke the last words.

Soon everyone had left the cargo bay, everyone except Adam.

Chapter 20

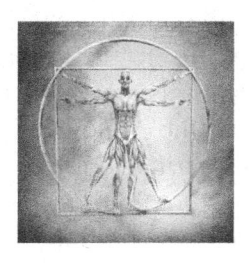

It's almost an impossible task to sneak up on someone when using a gravity drive; with the right sensors you can be detected for millions of miles away as you approach. So when the Juirean Fleet arrived near K'ly, alarms sounded at the pirate base and crews scrambled for their ships.

Pirates lived life on the edge, constantly looking over their shoulders for any real or perceived threats. One of their major concerns was that one of the more ambitious governments in The Fringe would try to gain political points by attacking their home base. So escape plans were honed and drills run until a pirate crew could have their ship up and in a well within ten minutes of an alarm.

And so like roaches when the lights come on, twenty-three pirate craft were bolting into space in a myriad of directions, following an escape plan designed to make it nearly impossible for an attacker to catch more than a few of the stragglers. Practice made perfect, and for the others—well the outcome was not so perfect.

Captains Jiden and Meldeon were on perimeter duty when the Juirean Fleet appeared. The assignment was a temporary punishment for their cut-and-run abandonment of the ship they'd attacked a few days earlier. Their real punishment would come when General Tarazi returned from Nimor....

Stationed about one-and-a-half million miles from K'ly, in the plane of the ecliptic, the two ship's captains spotted the massive gravity signatures moments before those on the planet below. Immediately on a link with each other, they quickly discussed their options.

Their first impulse was to run, just as their comrades were in the process of doing down on K'ly. But then they hesitated. They had just been fooled before by this very action. How would General Riyad react if they fell for the same ruse a second time?

So they stayed, charging up their weapons, battle crews at the ready, just in case the threat was real—this time.

One can only imagine the captains' shock when sixteen Juirean battle cruisers—the entire Fringe Fleet—came into extreme visual range, fanned out over ten-thousand miles so as to avoid overlapping wells. Now turning to run, the two pirate ships didn't make it very far before multiple bolts of intense plasma energy struck them from behind, taking out their maneuvering ports as well as most of their generator capacity.

Their ships remained in real space, drifting together, as two large battle cruisers slid in beside them and activated magnetic grapples. The rest of the fleet continued toward K'ly.

Jiden and Meldeon kept their links open as they expressed confusion as to why the Juireans had not simply blown them to dust. But they were still alive, and that had to count for something. So deciding that resistance was futile, they instructed their crews to stand down and allow the ships to be boarded without a fight.

It's a mistake to assume that a fleet of *Juirean* starships was manned solely by Juireans. In fact, out of the over fifteen-hundred beings occupying the fleet, there was only one Juirean aboard, and that was Fleet Commander Giodol Fe Bulen. Once the pirate ships were secured, their two captains were brought before the Juirean in his spacious stateroom aboard his Class-5 flagship.

Two heavily armed Rigorians forcefully dumped the captains into chairs before the commander, who remained seated behind a massive desk, casually stroking a rare MK-34 high-velocity bolt launcher that sat on the desk.

"I want information," Giodol began slowly. "Three days ago, a group of pirates attacked a ship in the Void near the Nimorian system. Do you have any knowledge of this action?"

The two captains looked at each other, then back to the Juirean. Meldeon spoke first: "There are a number of pirate ships here, My Lord. We're not aware of this particular attack." Both shifted nervously in the chairs.

The Juirean bore a dagger-look at them. "Are you sure? You've not heard anything of this attack?"

"Nothing, My Lord," Jiden offered.

The Juirean just nodded, then after a moment, lifted the MK-34 and sent a stun bolt into Jiden's chest. The captain was thrust backwards by the blast as the chair tumbled over. Hurt, but not severely injured, the two guards righted the chair and threw him back into it.

The Fleet Commander then took the weapon and dialed up the charge by three clicks before placing the weapon back on the desk. He returned his attention Meldeon.

"Again, I'll ask the question—"

"Yes! Yes, we know of the attack." Meldeon blabbered. "We are two of the three captains who were there. But we were just following orders, My Lord."

"That's not important. What *is* important is what you took from the ship before you departed."

The captains looked at each other again, confused, Jiden through spasms of burning pain. Then Meldeon spoke again, "My Lord, we took *nothing* from the ship. We didn't have time. Captain Angar had just finished his sweep for survivors when we were—when we departed."

The Juirean cocked his head and narrowed his eyes. "You took nothing? Are you sure?"

It was Jiden's turn to plead their innocence. "It was Captain Angar who went aboard. But we know for a fact that he did not take anything. We all expressed our frustration at having nothing to show for our efforts."

The Juirean began to nod his head. "That's very interesting. All I'm really concerned about is if anything was taken. And you both say there was nothing removed?"

The captains nodded emphatically. Then the Fleet Commander lifted the weapon again and blasted a hole through Meldeon's forehead. The level one bolt was clean and tight, and Meldeon simply slumped down in the chair, his head falling forward.

Stunned, Jiden began to tremble uncontrollably, his eyes wide with terror, saliva flowing from the corners of his mouth. The Juirean stared at him. "I'll ask the question again: Was anything taken from the ship?"

"No, My Lord! I swear as such. We took nothing!" He began to sob loudly.

"Now, now captain, pirates are not supposed to cry," Giodol said soothingly. "I believe you. I just had to be sure."

Jiden sat up a little straighter and wiped the moisture from his face. "Thank you, My Lord. I'm telling you the truth."

"I know you are." The Juirean then lifted the weapon and placed a bolt through Jiden's chest. Next, he pressed a button on his desk. "Open a link to the Overlord, immediately."

Chapter 21

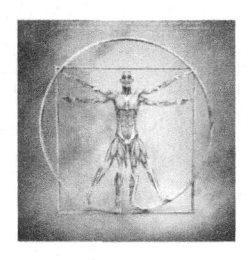

Moving quickly, Adam scanned the cargo hold for anything he could use to cut the bomb from his ankle. The cargo bay was filled with a plethora of tools, but most of them were robotic. From his brief time with the aliens, he had noticed that they weren't very coordinated, and this carried over to their use of tools as well.

However, Adam soon found what he was looking for. It was a thin length of wire with a corrugated edge. Taking a length of it, he threaded the wire between his ankle and the strap, and then he gripped the two ends of the wire with a couple of cloth rags. With purpose, Adam began to saw back and forth against the strap.

It wasn't long before metal dust began to accumulate on the chair. After about a minute he could see the wire making progress, cutting into the edges to the strap. This was going to work!

So he stopped.

It was too early in his captivity to chance having Riyad learn he'd escaped from the ankle bomb. And besides, Kaylor and Jym were still wearing theirs. He'd have to make sure the two aliens were free of their bracelets, too, before he took any action against Riyad and his pirates. He would pocket the wire for now, and then formulate a plan later.

Adam returned to his room. The journey to the asteroids had taken about five hours, so they should be arriving back at Nimor in another three. In the meantime, he had a lot of thinking to do.

Reclining on the bed, Adam began to run the conversation he'd had with Riyad back through his head. *So we're the Supermen of the galaxy?* Funny, he didn't feel like one. Yet he did have to admit that any preconceived notions he had about being awed by the great alien empire, and their vast superiority to Humanity, had been completely dashed by now. There was little out here that impressed him. Sure, they could travel between stars and they did have some pretty neat energy weapons. But beyond that, just about everyone he'd encountered had been a big letdown, including the almighty Juireans.

So was it possible that Riyad could actually return to Earth and conquer the planet using the Juirean technology? *Conquer* probably wasn't the right word. After all, what good would it do him to inherit a planet ravaged by war?

His plan would be more subtle. All he really had to do was allow the Juireans to learn of Earth's existence and its importance to the Klin. Then offering himself up as the most-qualified person to defend the planet against the alien threat, he could simply be appointed leader of the world. That would satisfy his ambition, but what of the Earth?

Could one planet really stand up against the combined might of the Juirean Expansion? Not likely, even with the help of the Klin. In fact, Adam had no idea who or what the Klin really were. Were they friend or foe? Would they use the Humans simply as fodder to further their own need for revenge? And were they any better than the Juireans?

These were serious questions for a 26-year-old Human from California.

Again, Adam let out a laugh. Was he really taking this line of thinking seriously? Could the activities aboard this tiny spaceship over the next day or so really impact the entire future history of the planet Earth?

Damn! This is some heavy shit, Adam thought.

He closed his eyes, and when he did, he saw a vision, an image of his wife Maria and her dark eyes filled with tears, her bottom lip trembling. She had tried to remain strong on the day he left for Afghanistan that last time, but it was getting so hard on both of them. No matter how hard you prepared for a moment like this, it was never as you planned. This time it had been even harder. Adam opened his eyes in an effort to make the vision go away; that line of thinking was just too painful to take.

He stared at the ceiling, having no idea how all of this was going to work out. But he knew one thing for certain: *He had to get home.* If there was any way possible, he would do it. And if Riyad had plans for involving Earth in a galactic war—which could bring harm to

Maria and Cassie, as well as to everyone else who was important to him—then he would have to be stopped.

Just then an announcement came over the ship's intercom, interrupting Adam's thoughts: "General Riyad, please come to the pilothouse immediately!" It was one of the terrorist's guards calling him.

Curious, Adam left his room and went to the pilothouse as well. He arrived the same time as Riyad.

"What is it?" the pirate leader demanded, anger and disgust displayed on his face and in his tone.

"We just received a link from your command ship. The K'ly base has been attacked by the Juirean Fleet!"

Adam saw Riyad's dark face grow a few shades deeper as veins in his neck began to protrude. Kaylor and Jym entered the room and Riyad spun to face them.

"See what your lies have done! The Juireans think we have the core so my base has been attacked. This is all because of you!"

Adam was half-expecting Riyad to draw his weapon and shoot both the aliens dead right there on the spot. Instead he turned to the guard. "Any word on the damage?"

The guard was listening on a headset. "So far, only five ships are unaccounted for. Your emergency evacuation plans were successful. The fleet is regrouping at the backup location."

"Who did we lose?"

"Filor, Caporian, Jiden, Sim and Meldeon," the guard reported.

"Jiden and Meldeon, good," Riyad said aloud. Then to the guard: "Send Captain Angar's ship to the rendezvous point with orders to coordinate all survivors. Backup supplies and weapons are to be distributed, and send out perimeter guards immediately. The Juireans will not rest until they have what they seek—and they did not find it on K'ly."

He turned to face Adam, fire in his eyes. "If you, or your alien friends, give me even one more problem, I will kill all of you without a second thought." He then stormed out of the room.

Chapter 22

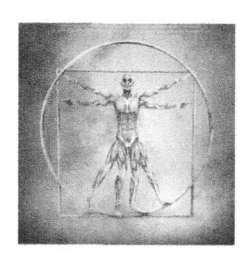

Adam spent the next couple of hours with Kaylor and Jym in the common room, sipping on carbonated drinks and chewing on some sort of granola-tasting cake. The aliens were scared to the point of incapacity; Jym had even thrown up a couple of times. Adam could sympathize with them, but he was also a little disappointed in their total lack of courage in the face of danger. Were these the same two aliens who had scared the pirates away from the Klin ship? He knew a showdown was coming with Riyad and his guards, and he dreaded the thought of having to rely on these two for help of any kind.

A guard appeared at the door and summoned them to the pilothouse.

"Take your seats," Riyad demanded of Kaylor and Jym. "We're at Nimor. Now take us to the Klin ship."

Kaylor seemed to be fighting the urge to say something. Finally he summoned the courage to speak. "The Ministry and the Juireans are probably going to be looking for us here. We haven't been gone very long," he said nervously.

"That's why we can't waste any more time. Just get us in and out as fast as possible."

Kaylor and Jym got very quiet and very serious. Through the open port, Adam could see the planet sweep into view, still impressed by the sight of another planet from space. But then he noticed the aliens begin to frantically work their controls, while repeatedly checking the view screens.

Riyad noticed this, too. "What's wrong?"

"The Klin ship ... it's not there." There was panic in Kaylor's voice.

Riyad moved closer, until he was looking over Kaylor's shoulder. "What do you mean it's not there?"

"These are the coordinates. It's where we left it in orbit by direction from the Ministry." Kaylor was near hysterics. "Honest! This is where we left it."

Riyad straightened up and stared out the viewport. "The Juireans have taken the ship away," he stated flatly.

Adam spoke up, "Where did they take it?"

"Probably to Melfora Lum," Riyad answered without turning. "That's the Juirean headquarters for The Fringe." Adam could tell that the terrorist was working multiple scenarios through in his head, as was Adam. They had the core, but it would do them no good without the Klin ship. And now that ship was headed for the Juirean stronghold in the region. How difficult would it be getting in and out of there? Adam was the rookie here; he had no idea.

Riyad turned to one of his guards. "Have the core transferred to my ship." He then turned to Adam: "I don't like you, Mr. Cain, and I certainly do not trust you. But I'm also not going to leave you here either. You're coming with me."

"What about us?" Jym asked, a little too loudly.

Riyad glared at him with a look that sent Jym recoiling back into his chair. "The two of you are the reason I'm in this mess in the first place. I'm afraid I don't have very good news for—"

Just then, a brilliant blue light filled the pilothouse. Everyone turned toward the viewport and saw three spacecraft appearing in front of them just as a massive blue bolt of energy deflected off one of their hulls. An elongated craft sweep into view from behind the *FS-475* and cut across the bow, just as another bolt of energy erupted from a point just above its pointed tip, targeted at the three approaching warcraft.

Almost simultaneously, three return bolts shot out from the attackers, striking the side of the elongated ship. Adam could see two of the bolts slide off the hull, while the third one scorched a path across the forward third of the ship.

Riyad turned to Kaylor. "Do you have any weapons on this tub?"

At first Kaylor didn't understand the question, but soon it dawned on him. "Nothing but a 45-ML launcher. It cannot puncture a battle hull."

Adam knew the fourth ship was Riyad's ride, and he also knew the ship was doomed. It had sped off to the right and was still barely visible when the three attackers changed course towards it, letting loose another barrage of blue balls of electricity as they turned. This time all three bolts penetrated the hull, and the ship exploded in a ball of yellow and green fire. Adam was astonished by the sudden evaporation of the explosion, as the great fireball flared briefly, and then vanished, as if sucked up by a giant vacuum. Yet even at this distance, Adam could still see pieces of the ship flying off in all directions.

Riyad stood stoically watching the scene before him unfold, while the three guards in the room appeared visibly shaken. Adam reasoned this was their ship, and now all of their shipmates were dead.

The three attackers changed course again and Adam could see bright flashes erupt from their sterns as they maneuvered closer to Kaylor's ship. It was apparent from their approach that they did not intend to fire.

A buzz sounded in the pilothouse; Kaylor reached forward on his console and threw a switch.

"This is the Nimorian Ministry Forces. You will prepare to be boarded."

All eyes turned to Riyad. "Do as they say," he commanded.

"What about the core?" Adam asked. "Are you going to let the Juireans have it?"

Just then a mischievous look crossed the pirate's face. "Don't worry," he said, as the corners of his mouth curved upward slightly. "We'll just have to take this fight to another venue."

Chapter 23

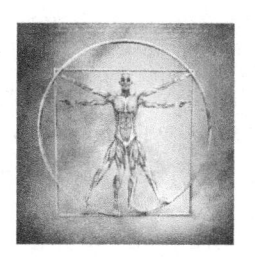

The *FS-475* was soon flooded with a myriad of aliens, all filled with a determined purpose. They quickly placed Riyad and his pirates in one of the extra staterooms under guard, while sequestering Adam, Kaylor and Jym in Kaylor's stateroom, also under guard.

Other pilots were brought in, and they set the ship on a course for Melfora Lum, a trip which would take about two days they were told. Then everyone settled into a tense routine. Food was brought and bathroom trips supervised. Adam and Riyad had no contact for the duration of the trip.

While in Kaylor's stateroom, Adam was able to remove all of their ankle bombs, much to their relief, especially the aliens. But now the question became: What to do with them now? They had not seen the trigger device removed from Riyad, but that could have happened by now. If not, then the bombs could go off at any time Riyad felt doing so would be to his advantage. And even one of the Nimorians could inadvertently trigger the device if it had been taken from him.

So during one of the bathroom runs, Adam hid the bombs in a towel and deposited them in a trash can in the head. Then asking for permission to dump the trash, Jym jettisoned the bombs out into the vastness of space.

Immediately, there was a profound change in the mood of Adam's two alien companions—at least up to the point when they remembered they were on the way to meet a Juirean Overlord ... a being who would decide the ultimate fate of them all.

The moment soon came when everyone was summoned to the airlock off the ship's cargo bay, and the four of them—Adam, Riyad, Kaylor and Jym—were transferred to a smaller shuttlecraft for the journey down to the surface of Melfora Lum. Riyad's fellow pirates appeared to have disappeared somewhere along the journey to the planet.

Through the viewports, Adam could see a sprawling city sweep up from below, complete with skyscrapers, paved roads and abundant traffic. *Now this was more like it*, Adam thought. This was a lot different from the Old West version of an alien city he'd experienced with the Nimorian city of Gildemont.

They landed in a parade field next to a massive pyramid-shaped building that easily measured a mile on each side. It soared forty stories tall and glowed a golden yellow color as the bronze-glass walls reflected the light from the setting Melforean sun. The prisoners were herded into the building under no fewer than fourteen guards.

The large entourage entered an even larger elevator; Adam once again marveled at the familiarity of it all. It was just a normal-looking elevator, yet he imagined the mechanism for moving the car up and down was probably a lot more high-tech than just cables and pulleys. At least that's what he hoped.

They entered an extremely large office, easily a hundred-feet-square, and lined with numerous full-size statues of exotic alien creatures, all garbed in bright uniforms and holding a variety of weapons. Over-sized plants were scattered throughout the room, and the troop had to wind their way through some of them before coming upon a massive desk, apparently carved from a single stone crystal. The desk was smooth along the front and back sides, but each of the opposing sides featured ornate carvings depicting various animals, all with savage, threatening expressions. The scene was clearly designed to intimidate.

And behind the desk sat the Juirean Counselor Deslor Lin Jul. He wore a slightly amused expression as the four prisoners were placed in chairs before the desk. This time the guards remained in the room, their beady yellow eyes unblinking as they never took them off of the prisoners. Adam could tell these guards were of a different caliber than the ones on Nimor. *Real pros.*

As he waited for the Counselor to begin speaking, Adam wondered when they would be meeting the Overlord. After all, Adam had already seen this movie....

Then the interview began.

The Juirean informed them that he was now aware of Riyad's identity, and had also taken note that he was of the same race as Adam. This had piqued his curiosity.

"I see we now have two of you, one a pirate captain and the other proclaiming ignorance as to how he came to be aboard the derelict ship. Does that seem inconsistent to either of you?"

"Let's cut the bullshit," Adam said. "We all know it was a *Klin* ship I was on."

The Juirean was sincerely taken aback. "So you know?" He seemed visibly upset. It was obvious this with information that was not for public consumption. Someone back on Nimor must have leaked the information.

"And this makes it all the more infeasible that you are simply an innocent victim of an abduction, with no knowledge of how or why you came to be aboard a *Klin* spacecraft."

He turned to address Riyad. "And you, of the same race, are a pirate leader and apparently quite adapt at our way of life. So which is it? Are you a primitive race, with no knowledge of the existence of The Expansion, or are you skilled warriors, as evidenced by your position with the pirates and your escape from the Nimorian jail?"

Neither Adam nor Riyad answered. Instead Riyad tilted his head toward Adam and said, "So this is a Juirean? I'm not impressed."

"That's just what I thought!" Adam replied emphatically.

The Juirean bristled. "Play your games as you wish, but I should tell you, we have recovered the Klin computer core."

Both Riyad and Adam were shocked. Before being boarded, Riyad had hidden the core within Kaylor's ship. They were hoping the Juireans still believed that the pirates had the core, and then when—not if—they could escape, they could recover the core and match it up with the systems aboard the Klin ship. In fact, Adam and Riyad were both quite ecstatic about getting both the core and the Klin ship back in close proximity to one another. But now....

"That's right," the Juirean said smugly, watching the expressions of the two Humans. "Your two captains were quite effective in convincing us that the pirates never did have the core in the first place. That only left the two of you," he said, addressing Kaylor and Jym. "After that, we didn't have too much difficulty finding the core aboard your ship during the trip to Melfora Lum."

Damn it! Now the Juireans are going to learn the location of Earth, Adam thought. *Where does that leave me now?*

Almost on queue, the Juirean spoke, "All of you are to be transported to the Klin ship to meet the Overlord. He is quite anxious to meet the two of you," he said addressing the two Humans. He turned to Kaylor and Jym. "As for the two of you, I have no idea what plans he has for you."

Adam saw Kaylor turn even paler than normal—and Jym fainted.

Chapter 24

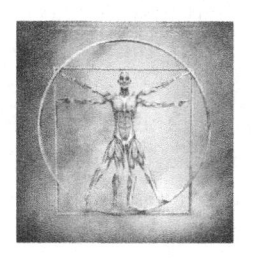

Two hours later, Adam was handcuffed and walking across a narrow metal plank in the umbilical corridor connecting the Counselor's private shuttle to the Klin ship. At the end of the plank, the group entered an airlock, and soon Adam found himself back in the same wide, curving corridor he had been in only six short days before.

Technicians had reestablished gravity, atmosphere and temperature, and even the air smelled like it had been disinfected, countering the stench of the dead bodies left by the pirates.

As he passed the wide window to the hiberpods room, he felt slightly nostalgic. He noticed that all the pods were all empty now, the dozens of dead Humans having been removed for disposal or for who knew what else.

They soon passed the wide stairway leading to the command dome and kept going. The party continued along the corridor, until it intersected with another corridor that cut through the center of the ship under the command dome. There were numerous doors on either side of the corridor, and Adam reasoned this must have been the living quarters for the crew.

A wide door slid open to his right, and the guards hustled them through, following the Counselor in his flowing and colorful capes.

The room was large, more deep than wide, with a large viewport at the opposite end. There was a living area off to the left, complete with a bed and working desk, partitioned off with half walls from the rest of the room. Along each wall were displayed colorful and strangely brilliant pictures that appeared almost to be alive. They were advanced 3-D images or holograms, and depicted landscapes of rolling hills, towering mountains and tranquil, azure blue seas. One picture was of a large obelisk surrounded by manicured grounds. And within the pictures were numerous beings, all the same tall silver creatures he'd seen when he'd first awakened on the ship. They were smiling and some were even holding children. Adam recognized the images immediately for what they were. These were scenes of home.

Adam noticed a figure standing near the photo of the obelisk, with his back to the group. A long, billowing crest of blue hair covered the head and cascaded down the back, and the creature wore a long purple cape.

Without turning, the Overlord spoke: "This is a vid of the Eternity Monument on Klinmon. It was destroyed nearly four thousand years ago ... but still they remember."

The Overlord turned, and Adam was immediately struck by the impossibly deep blue color of his eyes. They were almost hypnotic. The Overlord's face was similarly shaped as that of the Counselor's, but it appeared to have fewer creases around the eyes. *A young Juirean?* Adam wasn't sure, but thought it was a good bet.

The Counselor had taken a seat off to the right of the simple desk that was set near the rear viewport. He remained silent, as he waited for the Overlord to guide the conversation.

The Overlord swept his arm around the room. "This is all Klin. We are all standing in a memory, an ancient memory that has now been brought back to life." The Juirean's voice was almost singsong as he seemed enraptured by the moment. "This is living history. The Klin should not exist—but they *do*."

He walked over to the group and stopped in front of Adam. "They not only exist, but they appear to be thriving." The smell of the Juirean was of thick body odor, and his breath was a little sour. Adam did his best not to wince—at least not too much.

The Juirean continued. "I am Overlord Oplim Ra Unis. The four of you are all responsible, in one way or another, for this great moment in Juirean history. Because of your actions, I will be remembered forever in the chronicles of the Juirean people."

He walked over to the desk and leaned against it, facing the group. From the tone of the conversation, Adam almost felt as if the Juirean wanted to thank them for what they've done. Was that even possible?

He continued: "But do you know how close I came to not making this moment a reality?" His voice lowered. "Just having the Klin ship, without knowing the location of the Klin hiding place, would have caused more problems than it solved. It would simply have confirmed that the Klin still exist, and that they have advanced technology developed over thousands of years, technology and capabilities completely hidden from The Expansion. The result would have been Klin sightings all across the galaxy, a mass hysteria that would have undermined the Members' confidence in the Juirean Authority."

Then he stared at Kaylor. "And *you*—you had the computer core from the beginning."

Kaylor's eyes grew wide with terror, as Jym tried to slip in behind him, hiding from the steely gaze of the Overlord.

At that moment, a communicator on the Counselor's belt buzzed, distracting the Overlord momentarily. The Counselor quickly answered, whispered into the device, and then he stood and moved next to the Overlord.

"My Lord, the technicians have tried all they can to decipher the information from within the core, but there is a compatibility issue. They believe the core must be linked to its original system." There was a slight concern in his voice.

The Overlord firmed his jaw, and then instructed the Counselor to have the core transferred to the ship immediately. He stood silently for a long moment, looking into the room without seeing. All the others stood silently, shifting nervously. The Overlord was used to doing things in his own time.

Finally, he took a deep breath and said, "Now you see why we have purged all evidence of the discovery of this ship. The only beings that know of the ship's true identity are here in this room. Only *after* I have learned the location of the Klin hiding place, and purged The Expansion of their plague, will I let the rest of the galaxy know what I have done."

After being confined to a small room near the Overlord's chambers for an hour or so, the four of them were eventually herded up to the command dome where the Overlord and his Counselor were waiting. The core had arrived, and technicians were preparing to install it back into the equipment tower. Adam noticed Riyad separate himself from him and the two aliens, to stand closer to the Juireans. The rest of the room was crowded with guards and various technicians.

The last time Adam was in this room was when Kaylor had shot him, and the wound on his chest, as well as the one on his head from the collision with the bulkhead, still had not healed completely. Adam noticed that Kaylor and Jym were becoming ever-more agitated, almost panicky. They had been petrified with fear for quite a while now, but this was different.

The technicians lifted the core and struggled to get it lined up in the opening in the equipment tower. Then it slid in. Immediately, three steady orange lights above the core opening changed to yellow and began to flash in sequence.

Kaylor and Jym literally ran for the exit, but were quickly subdued by the guards. The Juireans didn't notice the commotion; instead, they had turned their attention to the command consoles as a screen suddenly flashed to life. A technician sat down at the console and began to type on the keyboard before him. Data began to stream across the screen. The Juireans leaned in closer.

Adam was curious, too, but of course, he couldn't read any of the data. What really piqued his interest, however, was how strange Kaylor and Jym were acting....

"There!" the Overlord yelled, pointing his finger at the screen. "Stop," he commanded to the technician. "Surrender your seat and leave the room."

When the seat was empty, the Counselor slipped into it. Only the two Juireans could now see the screen. They began to read intently.

Kaylor grabbed Adam's sleeve. "We have to leave!" he whispered to Adam.

"What? We can't leave."

"We have to!"

Adam shrugged off Kaylor's grasp and returned his attention to the Juireans. If they learned the location of Earth, they might reveal something that Adam could use later—if there was to be a later. He couldn't read the screen, even if he could see it, but he could *listen* in on their conversation.

"Amazing." the Counselor was saying. *"Annan."*

"Yes, but that is not what concerns me the most," said the Overlord. "Look what it says about these Humans...."

Both the Juireans turned to look at Adam and Riyad, who in unison backed away quickly, trying to look as innocent as possible. *Did the Juireans look ... scared?* Adam thought. Then they turned back to the screen.

"There! That's it—" the Overlord said.

A heartbeat later, Riyad shoved a shoulder into Adam's chest, sending him crashing into Kaylor, Jym and the guards behind them. They all tumbled to the floor in a heap. Next, Riyad kicked the Counselor in the ribs, and grabbed the much-taller Overlord around the neck from behind, pulling him backwards.

Guards rushed into the room, weapons drawn. Riyad swung the Overlord in front of him for cover, and the guards hesitated. The pirate backed further into the room, almost disappearing from Adam's view due to the curvature of the room within the circular ship. Then with his free hand, Riyad reached down and flipped his belt buckle inside out, revealing the trigger device for the ankle bombs! He grinned at Adam—and then pushed a button on the device at the same time he ducked around the equipment tower.

But nothing happened.

A few seconds later, Riyad, with the Overlord still firmly in his grasp, peaked around the corner. Adam had regained his feet, and seeing Riyad's dark eyes staring at him, he pulled his pant leg up to reveal a bare ankle.

A look of exasperation came over Riyad's face. Then a toothy smile stretched across his face. Riyad gave Adam a wink, and then moved back out of sight, dragging the Overlord with him.

Guards rushed past Adam, nearly knocking him over, and went to help the Counselor to his feet. Others headed after Riyad, who had exited the command room through a secondary doorway.

Adam felt a strong tug on his arm. "Come Adam, we *must* go—now!" Kaylor had an absolutely terrified look on his face.

Using the confusion left over from Riyad's abduction of the Overlord, Adam sent an elbow into the jaw of the one remaining guard standing between them and the stairway out of the command room. He scooped up the guard's weapon, and the three of them bounded down the stairs and into the wide corridor. Three more guards ran past them and up the stairs, ignoring them completely. It seemed that rescuing the Overlord was of a greater priority than subduing the three of them.

And so they ran, back down the corridor, past the hiberpod room and into the umbilical tube. The hatch to the Counselor's ship was still open and they shot through it, Adam leading the way. Finding no one aboard, they quickly located the pilothouse and Kaylor fell into the pilot's seat a seat, punching buttons as he did so.

"What the hell's going on?" Adam yelled, as Kaylor fingered a switch that closed the outer door to the ship. Next, Kaylor grabbed the control stick and sent the craft tearing away from the umbilical.

"The bomb!" Jym answered.

"What bomb?"

Kaylor cranked the stick to the left, and Adam could see the large Klin ship began to shrink away quickly.

"The nuclear bomb that's aboard the Klin ship," Kaylor said, as he switched the screens to an aft view. The Klin ship was now about the size of the full moon and rapidly shrinking as the distance between the two craft increased.

"There's a nuke aboard the ship? How do you know?"

"The core was hooked to a self-destruct mechanism," Kaylor explained. "When I removed the core originally it activated the countdown. I was trying to disarm the bomb when you first attacked me."

"So, why is this a problem now? You obviously *did* deactivate it."

"The lights," Kaylor said, not taking his eyes from the view screen. The Klin ship had disappeared from view by now. "Before I removed the core, the lights were orange. When I removed it, the lights turned yellow and began to oscillate, just as they're doing now."

"But why would the self-destruct activate when the core was returned?"

"Because I *reversed* the controls. The device thinks the core has been removed, again. We have about seven minutes to get to a safe distance."

Without further comment, Adam joined Kaylor and Jym in their silent vigil at the view screen....

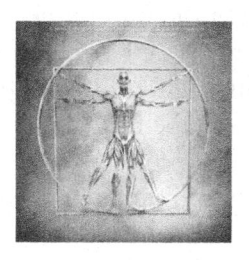

Chapter 25

Riyad pulled the struggling Overlord through the side door to the command room and dragged him down a hallway. Although he was unarmed, Riyad did have the most valuable hostage in the entire Fringe.

He had planned for the ankle bombs to go off and take out most of the guards, and then in all the confusion he could have easily slipped away with the Overlord virtually unseen. But that didn't happen. Now he knew he only had a few seconds to extract the information he needed from his hostage. After that he could dispose of the Overlord and fight his way off the ship. And from the reactions of the two Juireans, he was sure they had learned the locations of both the Klin hideout and of Earth. The key to his entire future was held in his strong right arm as he pulled the Overlord further down the hallway.

Guards could be seen cautiously moving down the hallway toward them, safely keeping their distance. All of a sudden the ship rumbled, and Riyad felt an explosion vibrate through its metal structure. Almost immediately, he heard the sounds of plasma bolts charging the air. The guards seemed confused, as some broke off to disappear down the hallway.

Just then a stream of high-intensity electric bolts shot over his head from behind him and toward the guards. The guards returned the fire, and Riyad now found himself caught in the middle of a firefight.

He dragged the Overlord through a doorway on his right and threw him to the floor. There was a battle going on in the hallway, and this could be his opportunity to interrogate the Overlord. Riyad straddled the Overlord, grabbing him firmly around the neck. The eyes of the Overlord were wide, as he struggled vainly to escape, but Riyad was able to easily kept the him pinned to the floor.

"You found the location of Earth. Give me the coordinates." Riyad demanded, squeezing tighter on the alien's neck.

The Overlord tried to shake his head, but Riyad's grip restricted the movement.

"I will not," the Overlord managed to say through gritted teeth.

"Then I will crush the life out of you with my bare hands. You have about two seconds to tell me!" He squeezed even tighter.

"Yes! Ecliptic plane ... minus 4, section 21 ..." the Overlord strained to say. Riyad could feel his heart begin to race—

Just then, Riyad heard a strange scraping sound on the metal floor of the hallway outside the room. The sound was growing louder. Riyad looked over at the open doorway—just in time to see a small, puck-size disk come sliding up and stop right at the doorway.

Riyad's eyes grew wide. It was a grenade, like those his pirates used when boarding a hostile ship!

He rolled off the Overlord and further into the room, just as the bomb exploded. He felt a hot searing pain across his right side — and then darkness enclosed him.

Counselor Deslor found the unconscious Overlord in a side room, bloody, but alive. Guards swept in and helped their leader to a nearby couch, just as he was regaining his senses.

"Where are the Humans?" he asked the Counselor through the pain.

"I do not know. We are searching the ship."

The Overlord reached up and grabbed the Counselor's cloak. "Open a link to the Fleet Commander—now!"

"Of course, my Lord. But shouldn't you receive medical assistance?"

"Only after I speak with Giodol."

The Counselor spoke to a guard, who then hurried out of the room. Moments later, a tech arrived with a portable transmission unit. He placed the device on a table at the end of the couch, and after a few moments, stepped away so the two Juireans could operate the communicator. Deslor sent everyone out of the room.

The pain woke Riyad from his blissful sleep. He became aware of people around him, and he opened his eyes to find he was lying across a console chair in the pilothouse of a shuttlecraft. Through groggy and filmy eyes, he could see Angar seated at the controls, the blackness of space showing through the front viewport. His body ached all over, and suspected his right arm was badly damaged from the throbbing pain emanating from that part of his body. He groaned, and instantly several people were at his side, helping him sit up in the seat.

Angar turned to face him, a large, satisfied grin on his face. "I'm so glad to see you're awake, My General," he said. "The meds should make you feel better pretty soon."

"Where am I?" Riyad managed to force out of his dry throat.

"You're in a shuttle. We're almost back to my ship."

"How…how did I get here?"

"We rescued you." Angar's voice was proud and animated. "I brought a boarding party and pulled you out. You're safe now."

Memory began to surface in Riyad, and he soon remembered sitting atop the Juirean Overlord, hearing him recite the coordinates of planet Earth. And then an explosion!

"You idiot!" Riyad screamed at Angar, as loudly as he could manage.

Angar recoiled with a shocked look. "My General?"

Riyad managed to stand, cradling his broken right arm in his left. Between gritted teeth and spasms of pain he said, "I was about to learn the location of my homeworld—until you interfered."

Angar's jaw was slack, his eyes wide. He didn't know what to say, so Riyad stepped into the silence. "Turn around. We have to go back."

"But General, we … we can't—"

"Do it, damn it!"

Angar sat back down in the pilot's seat and cranked the stick over. The star field changed ahead of them, but they were so far out that the Klin ship was not visible. Riyad stood weakly behind the pilot seat, overflowing with anger. He was so close! The Juirean had been in the process of telling him where his home was located. He had half the coordinates: Ecliptic minus 4, sector 21. Another second and he would have had it all.

The link to the Fleet Commander was established, and Oplim and the Deslor moved closer to the small screen on the unit. "Are you injured, My Lord?" he asked, seeing the bloody and battered Overlord. This was unheard of. No one in his memory had ever even struck a Juirean, let alone injured one as badly as his Overlord.

"Listen to me, this is important." the Overlord said. *"The Klin exist!"*

The Commander's mouth fell open as his eyes grew wide. "Are you sure?" He was so shocked by the statement that he abandoned all decorum with his superior.

"Yes, Commander. They have a secret base in the area. But that is not our biggest threat."

"What ... what could be worse?"

"It's a race of beings called *Humans*. I will give you the coordinates to their planet. Then Commander, you must assemble your fleet and—"

The Fleet Commander saw his screen go completely blank, no static, no ghost images. He pressed the controls to regain the link, but nothing happened.

After a few more tries, he called in a technician. Another few minutes went by while the terrified technician tried in vain to reestablish the connection. Finally, he had to tell the Commander that there was nothing wrong with his equipment.

There was simply nothing left to link to....

The blast first appeared as tiny, yet brilliant dot against the star field. Adam and his two alien companions watched in horror as the dot grew almost instantly to fill half the sky. They turned away to shield their eyes, before the view screen darkened to lessen the light intensity inside the pilothouse.

A nuclear explosion in space is quite different than one within an atmosphere. The fire was not as intense from of the lack of oxygen to feed the flame, and there is no shockwave from the compressed air. But the radioactivity from the explosion created an almost perfect sphere of light, as the force expanded outward, equally in all directions. But what was most startling to Adam were the bolts of electric blue and yellow lightning that shot out from the point of origin. It reminded him of one of those static electricity globes he used to see at Spencer's Gifts at the mall. The ribbons were beautiful and filled most of their view, traveling away on their own, slowly losing intensity as the minutes passed.

Chapter 26

Riyad cradled his shattered right arm and fought the wave of nausea flowing through his body. He had no idea what had happened to the Klin ship. Had it been destroyed from the outside, maybe by the Klin themselves? Or was there a bomb aboard, a booby-trap of some kind? Either way, he was beyond anger, literally shaking from hatred for all things alien.

His vision had been so real—and he had been so close. *Riyad Tarazi, ruler of the planet Earth!* And now his vision had evaporated in an instant, along with the computer core and the Klin ship, all in a fireball of splitting atoms and radioactive debris.

Through the viewport, he watched as the last of remnants of the explosion dissipated into the nothingness of space above Melfora Lum—sparking ribbons of blue and yellow radiation. And then there was nothing, just the myriad of steady lights dotting the blackness of space.

But that's not exactly true, he thought, as a glimmer of an idea swelled up from his gut. *I now know that the Klin exist. They not only know the location of Earth, but I sincerely believe they're building an army of Humans, probably somewhere right here in The Fringe.*

With a new-found determination borne of hatred, as well as his lust for power, Riyad swore then and there that he now had a new purpose in life. He would rounded up the scattered remains of his pirate fleet, and then he would spend every waking hour, every ounce of his being, on the singular quest of finding the Klin hideout and their Human army.

He *would* make his vision come true. He knew now that it was possible. He would find the Klin, and he would return to Earth. And from then on, his homeworld would never be the same....

On the other side of Melfora Lum, Adam stood at the viewport of the *FS-475*, watching as the last remnants of the nuclear blast evaporated into ribbons of sparking blue and yellow electricity. He couldn't believe it. He had been so close to finding his way home.

In reality, he didn't care what happened to the Klin—or to anything else for that matter—in this nightmare universe he now occupied. All he'd ever wanted to do was get back home.

And now what was he to do....

Kaylor and Jym stood behind him, not knowing what to say. Adam finally spoke without turning, "I guess I'm stuck here now. There will be no joyous homecoming for Adam Cain in the foreseeable future." He turned to face the two aliens. "But it looks like the two of you are off the hook for now. The Juirean did say no one else knew about the ship and about the Klin other than a small handful of people. Now most of them are gone, all except us."

There was an awkward moment of silence. Then Kaylor asked, "What will you do now?"

Adam just shook his head. "Well, if I'm going to be here for a while, the first thing I need to do is find a way to make a living. The two of you can't keep carrying me forever."

Kaylor nodded vigorously, much to Adam's surprise. "What were you trained to do on your planet ... on Earth?"

Adam thought for a moment. He knew the long answer, but the time didn't seem appropriate to go into detail. Finally, he simply said, "I was a trained killer."

Both Kaylor and Jym recoiled slightly from the answer. They had held their suspicions, and now it was confirmed.

Seeing the disgust on the faces of the aliens, Adam explained further, "I was in the military, a warrior I guess you could say."

This seemed to bring them a degree of relief, but then Jym blurted out, "Maybe you can go to work for the gangs—*as an assassin!*"

Kaylor jabbed him in the ribs, shooting him a stern look.

But Adam wasn't offended. In fact, he gave them both a sly smile and said, "So, I could kill aliens for a living? *I could get used to that!*

The End

The Fringe Worlds

Book One of
The Human Chronicles Saga

Next up in
The Human Chronicles Saga:

Alien Assassin
(Available Now)

In the exciting continuation of **The Human Chronicles Saga**, ex-Navy SEAL Adam Cain finds himself attempting to make a living the best he can in the alien universe he's been dropped into—as an assassin! After all, with his kick-ass attitude and instinctive hatred for aliens, he's a natural at it.

As a Human among aliens, he's stronger, faster and tougher than just about everyone—and everything—he encounters. In this reality—**Adam is the Superman**.

Alien Assassin is a whirl-wind adventure of incredible space battles, shoot-outs with galactic criminals, and even a love interest that is ... well, a little different. And as all this is going on, the political forces of revenge and 4,000-year-old grudges converge on The Fringe Worlds. But even as galactic forces close in on Adam and his gang, there's one message that all the aliens begin to grasp: **Don't mess with the HUMANS!**

> Don't wait. Pick up your copy of *Alien Assassin* today.
> *And let the adventure continue...*

Please see this exciting excerpt from

Alien Assassin

Book Two of The Human Chronicles Saga....

Adam Cain is an alien with an attitude.
His story continues...

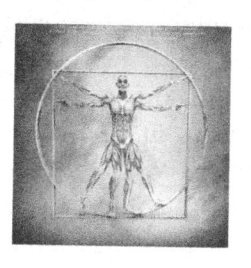

Chapter 1

*A****dam Cain had an alien to kill...***
...Yet before setting out on the mission, his professional training dictated that he take inventory of his equipment and run a weapon's check....

Adam was in a pressurized hotel room in the Hildorian city of Jaxas, and spread out on the bed before him was a full array of energy weapons and other tactical gear. Although the tactics and strategies he'd learned during his formal U.S. Navy SEAL training had very little carryover into his present occupation, the habits developed during those years were hard to break. So with methodical precision, Adam went down the mental checklist and triple-checked his weapons.

His formidable weapons cache ranged from the standard MK-17 and XF Flash Rifle, all the way up to his prized MK-47 High Energy Bolt Launcher. The '47 had cost him nearly an entire contract fee, but it had been well worth it. Being the top-of-the-line for handguns, the weapon boasted a standard level-one charge of twenty bolts, and its targeting computer carried the fastest rating in its class.

Personally, Adam never used the targeting assist, but just carrying the weapon often gave those who sought to challenge him second thoughts.

Honestly, Adam didn't really care if they challenged him or not. He would kill anything that walked, slithered or crawled in this godforsaken galaxy. In fact, Adam often referred to himself as *The Exterminator*, and every time he did a hit, he felt about as much remorse as The Orkin Man did when he wiped out a colony of termites back home.

Adam lifted the '47, feeling its weight and the comfort of the grip in his hand. All his pistol grips were customized, as was the stock on his Xan-Fi Flash Rifle. With over 8,000 species in the Juirean Expansion, weapons manufacturers had to provide an extensive selection of grips and stocks to fit the variety of hands, tentacles and even robotic nerve attachments of their customers. Luckily for Adam, Human-style hands were quite common. Even still, he chose to have his stocks and grips molded to fit his hands exactly, providing even more control and confidence than was probably necessary. But Adam Cain was a professional, and nothing but the best would do.

For the past three days, Adam had donned the uncomfortable pressure suit and breathing attachment, and scouted the mark. His name was Kunnlar Bundnet, a high-level gang leader who had offended an even higher-level crime boss—and now had to pay the price. As it was back on Earth, most gang hits were within and between the gangs themselves. Adam didn't really care. As long as they paid, he would kill. After all, it was the only thing he was really good at.

Satisfied that all was in order, Adam gathered up the tools of his trade and placed them in one of the backpacks on the bed, while reserving the '47 for this oiled leather holster. He then strapped the clear plastic breathing cup over his nose, and scooped up the other knapsack from the bed. Lastly, Adam placed the camouflage boonie hat atop his head—the trademark of his SEAL persona—and cinched up the cord under his chin.

It was game time.

Bundnet lived in a fortified compound on a hill about 30 klicks outside of town. Adam drove the rented transport to within a kilometer of the house, and after applying streaks of dark green grease to his face, he slung the flash rifle across his back and secured four slide grenades to the MK's utility belt. And then with the small knapsack secured across his left shoulder, he set off for the compound, covering the remaining distance in about a minute, through a combination of jogs and long leaps in the weak gravity.

In fact, gravity was an integral part of his attack plan. Rated at just .69 of standard, Adam estimated the surface gravity of Hildoria to be a little over half that of Earth's. That was one of the reasons the atmosphere was so thin and the air pressure too low for him to function without the light pressure suit. It also produced natives who were all well-over two meters tall with huge, barrel chests. Apparently it required large lungs to inhale enough of the thin oxygen to survive....

The singular yellow sun had set by the time Adam reached the compound, and a deep darkness descended on the landscape of thick woods and bristled bushes, yet the compound itself stood out like a beacon. It was illuminated by numerous floodlights, and with at least a dozen heavily-armed guards patrolling both sides of the surrounding wall. The place was hard to miss.

His sources had informed him that Bundnet may have been forewarned of the impending hit. This didn't concern Adam too much—it simply came down to whether or not this would be a surgical strike or an all-out scorched-earth campaign. To *The Exterminator*, either way would get him paid.

Crouching in a clump of bushes at the tree line, Adam watched as the first set of guards covered their route, flash rifles of their own held casually at their sides. Once they passed, he dashed off toward the wall, to a point he had selected earlier as his best point of entry.

Leaning against the warm stone surface, Adam estimated the height of the wall to be about five or six meters. *Now comes the fun part*, he thought with a smile. And then in a move that would have made any NBA center green with envy, he jumped straight up, enjoying the momentary sensation of flying, and easily reached the top of the wall with his outstretched arms. Then with a quick, fluid motion, he swung himself over the top and descended—essentially in slow motion—to the ground below.

Immediately, alarms began to blare, as motion sensors along the wall were tripped. Adam scrambled to a dark patch of trees and vegetation and lay on the cool, moist ground, watching as more guards rushed toward the clearing between the wall and the house. Each held flash rifles, and their large size and bulging chests produced a menacing, ominous scene.

Removing the small knapsack from his shoulder, Adam quickly released the binding cord and opened the pouch. With angry growls, two furry creatures—looking like large squirrels with spiked tails—shot out of the bag and ran off into the clearing. The guards spotted the animals almost immediately, and began chasing after them in a vain attempt to corral the elusive creatures.

As planned, Adam watched as one of the guards placed a communicator to his mouth, and a few moments later the alarms were silenced. The obedient rodents continued their flight to freedom across the field and away from Adam's position, with the guards following closely behind.

Soon Adam saw his opportunity, and in a low crouch, took off for the house. Without breaking stride, he vaulted to the top of a small pagoda-type structure, and then onto the roof of the main building. He fell in behind a towering chimney stack, and waited to see if anyone had spotted his movement. Satisfied that he was unseen, he proceeded along the roof, until he came to a large skylight made up of numerous individual glass panels. A dim light filtered up from a single source in the room below.

Adam peered over the edge of the skylight and saw a large bedroom below; an expansive bed to one side, a set of dresser drawers against one wall and a wooden writing desk against another. And seated at the desk was Kunnlar Bundnet, leaning forward slightly, his arms on the desk.

Anticipating that the skylight frame would be wired for security, Adam removed a roll of tape from his bag, and quickly and quietly covered one of the glass panes with a large 'X,' leaving a rise of tape at the center. Next he took out a pen-laser, a special one with a muted tip, and began to silently cut through the glass along its edge. Then holding the rise of tape at the center, Adam lifted the glass away from the skylight frame and set it to one side.

Next he stood and withdrew his MK-47, and with a deep breath, stepped through the skylight opening to begin a slow-motion drop into the room below.

Landing with a muffled sound, Adam crouched on one knee, pointing his weapon at Bundnet's back, fully expecting the crime lord to spin around in his chair toward the sound. But no movement came.

Cautiously, he moved closer to Bundnet, weapon at his cheek, sighting along the barrel. Still no movement. He slid up to the side of the desk, and leaned forward to look into Bundnet's face.

The large, beady alien eyes were wide open, with a look of sheer terror frozen in them. And across his neck was a smooth razor cut, filled with dark, coagulated blood that had soaked into the front of his gold and green shirt.

But what surprised Adam the most—*this was not Bundnet!*

Adam sensed another presence in the room—

He dove to his left, just as a bolt of electric-blue energy slammed into the desk, sending splinters of wood trailing after him. Rolling on his shoulder, Adam came up on one knee, just as a large, boxy figure appeared out of the shadows near the bedroom door. He leveled the MK-47 and fired. Instantly, a shimmering wave of blue light enveloped the figure, and then quickly dissipated. *A diffusion screen!* His sidearm would be unable to penetrate the shield; he would need something larger—like the flash rifle he carried across his back.

Yet before Adam could un-sling the rifle, the large figure lumbered further into the room, and stopped. It made no further threatening moves, so Adam slowly stood to face his attacker.

It was Kunnlar Bundnet, very much alive, and encased in an exosuit. He had an MK-17 leveled at Adam—*and he was smiling.*

Hildorians often wore exosuits when off-planet, to help compensate for the heavier gravity they encountered on nearly every other world in The Fringe. The suits were mechanical transports, attached to the limbs of the wearer, providing added strength and support for their brittle-boned bodies. They also carried their own power supply, to which Bundnet had apparently linked a diffusion screen. Diffusion screens were very basic shields against smaller bolt launchers, yet because they often required an external power source, they were impractical for personal protection—unless you were wearing an exosuit.

"So you must be the assassin Amick sent to kill me," Bundnet stated in a rough, gravelly voice. Adam couldn't help but notice how the movements of his mouth were not in sync with the words he heard, a common occurrence with the translation bug implanted behind his ear. This oddity was something Adam had never gotten used to.

Adam did not answer. Instead he glanced around when he heard heavy metal shutters quickly lower over the windows to the bedroom, effectively trapping him in the room with the mechanically-enhanced Hildorian crime boss.

"Yes, I've been expecting you," Bundnet said. "You see, I have my sources as well, and I can assure you that plans are in the works that will have Amick paying the ultimate price for sending you against *me*."

Adam heard the servos whine, as Bundnet stepped further into the room, until he was only a few meters away. With the alien already standing well over two meters tall, now encased in the exosuit Bundnet presented a truly intimidating figure, towering by a good meter or more over Adam.

"I've heard of you," the alien continued, confident in his control of the situation. "At times, I have even considered enlisting your services for my own ends."

"You should have," Adam finally said. "You would have lived longer."

Adam saw a look of confusion cross the alien's face. "You don't seem to realize the position you are in, assassin. You're as good as dead, and I have options as to how I will bring about your final demise. I can either shoot you—or I can rip you apart limb by limb, while reveling in the agony you will be experiencing. Personally, I prefer the second option. It will bring me more satisfaction hearing your screams."

Adam just smiled, which did nothing to fit into the Hildorian's vision he had of this moment. *Here we go again*, Adam thought. And then aloud: "Bring it on, asshole!"

Knowing that the weapon he held was useless against the diffusion screen, Adam reeled back and heaved the '47 at Bundnet. With the weapon carrying no electrical charge of its own, it passed through the screen as if it wasn't there, and struck Bundnet's hand with the force of a sledgehammer, knocking his own weapon away.

Bundnet roared with anger and pain; he lurched forward, swinging his right arm as he did so, with the exosuit adding extra quickness and agility. Still, it wasn't enough. Adam blocked the blow easily, and then lifted the entire mechanical/alien contraption off the floor and shoved it to his right. The suit was able to maintain balance, but Bundnet now found himself twisted around, with Adam behind him.

Rather than attack, Adam simply waited for his opponent to spin back around. The smile had vanished from Bundnet's face.

"You missed," Adam said, through a toothy grin of his own.

The Hildorian literally growled at him, displaying a double row of long, sharp teeth. Bundnet lunged again, yet this time a mechanical hand was able to grasp Adam's left bicep, sending a spasm of pain through his arm and shoulder. Adam reached across with his free hand and ripped the clamp from his arm, breaking the thin metal from its joints.

Bundnet screamed in agony, as his own flesh and blood hand was twisted and bones snapped. But he was still able to counter with a swipe of the other mechanical arm. Adam was struck hard against the side of the head and knocked to his knees, temporarily stunned. Bundnet used the opportunity to step forward, crashing his metal-encased left leg forcefully into Adam's chest.

Adam flew backwards in the light gravity and landed heavily on the wooden chest next to the bed. Bundnet ran forward.

Quickly regaining his senses, anger flared in Adam. He pushed off of the chest, and the two combatants crashed into each other in the center of the room. Adam scampered on top of the suit's metal frame and began to rip at the upper cage above Bundnet's head. Metal bars broke easily from their joints, as Bundnet's mechanical arms flailed wildly, trying to pull Adam from atop the cage. Then the assassin dropped in behind Bundnet and ripped the power cords from the battery pack.

Instantly, the servos fell quiet, and Bundnet found himself trapped in the suit, only able to move it with his own feeble strength. He stopped struggling, and watched as Adam moved slowly back in front of him.

Adam just shook his head. "You don't have any idea what you're up against, do you?" The alien's bottom lip was trembling. He didn't answer.

"This is what I do. *I kill aliens for a living.* And I'm very good at it—"

Adam then shot out with his right arm, clamping his hand around the alien's neck. He squeezed, and could feel—and hear—the crunching of cartilage as the alien's windpipe collapsed. In another moment, it was all over.

Adam Cain, Alien Assassin, had successfully fulfilled yet one more contract.

After a brief moment of contemplation, Adam quickly gathered up his backpack and recovered his MK-47—just as he became aware of the wailing of alarms outside the building. How long they had been going off he couldn't tell; his mind had been on other matters.

But Adam didn't panic. Yes, he had been discovered, but all he had to do now was get out of the compound, and that he had no doubt he could do.

The windows of the bedroom were shuttered and the exterior walls of the building were made of stone, so his only escape route was through the bedroom door. Gripping his '47 firmly in his right hand, he flung the door open and immediately came face-to-face with two guards, just as shocked to see him as he was to see them. With lightning-quick reactions, Adam blasted the first one through the chest with a bolt from the MK, and then swung his left fist at the second guard. Much to Adam's surprise, his fist sank completely into the guard's skull and exited out the other side, effective hooking the alien's head onto Adam's forearm, all in a bloody spray of brains and shattered bone material.

Damn! What else could go wrong?

Just then, a whole array of bolt streaks filled the hallway, as yet another group of armed guards appeared to his right. Adam needed a new exit strategy....

One of the good things about a low-gravity world was that construction did not have to be as strong and sturdy as one with more gravity. Even though atoms were atoms everywhere in the universe, the strength of the compounds and building materials varied from world to world. So what Adam had discovered about construction on Hildoria—and Bundnet's house in particular—was that everything was essentially built of material about as strong as balsa wood and popsicle-sticks.

So Adam leapt across the hallway, through the blaze of energy bolts, and smashed through the opposite wall with little effort, dragging the dead alien on his arm as he did so.

Stumbling through a fallen metal shelving unit, Adam found himself in the home's kitchen area, and as he ran between rows of preparation tables, he continued to try and shake the stuck alien off his arm. At that moment, he could hear the words of Riyad Tarazi echoing in his head, as the Human leader of the Fringe Pirates had told him how Humans were the *Supermen* of the galaxy. As he feverishly tried to dislodge the lifeless guard from his arm, Adam was pretty sure Clark Kent never had to deal with a problem like this....

Finally, the lifeless alien slipped from his arm and Adam was able to holster the '47 and pull the flash rifle from across his back. As he did so, he whipped the weapon around, spraying a barrage of bolts at the guards entering through the hole in the wall he'd just made. Then he continued the arc, blasting more holes in the walls, cabinets and other aliens—kitchen staff he reckoned—in a full circle around him. The sights and sounds were deafening, of crumbling ceilings, burning wallboard and wailing creatures. Then fires began to flare up, from grease, fabric and burning wood. It all added to the confusion Adam was hoping for.

Soon he was out of the kitchen and blasting his way across a large dining area. He was surprised to see even more guards rush headlong into the hall, wondering just how many of them Bundnet had on the grounds. There seemed to be a lot more than when he'd reconned the compound over the past few days.

Oh well, just more score to rack up....

Then to his shock and surprise, Adam felt a heavy thud hit his back. He flew forward and fell, sliding several meters on the polished stone floor. He knew he'd taken a hit to the back, but was relieved to find that his own makeshift diffusion screen had apparently worked. Since flash bolts from all the various energy weapons they carried were made up of concentrated balls of electricity, Adam had fashioned a series of wires sewn onto the exterior of the pressure suit he wore. Not as strong or long-lasting as a full-fledged diffusion shield, his experiments had shown however that the electric bolts would dissipate along the wires, heating them up and melting the wires, but also lessening the impact of the hit. The concussion still knocked him off his feet, but that was about the extent of the damage. Of course he also knew that the wire mesh was only good for one bolt. The next one could prove fatal.

Rolling on his back as he slid along the floor, Adam aimed the flash rifle between his legs at the three guards who had taken up positions behind him. His aim was true, and the bolts from the rifle had a devastating effect on the thin-boned Hildorians. Then he was on his feet again and running for the main entrance of the home.

The ornate, double front doors were made of a metal of some kind, so instead of barreling through them, Adam jumped and crashed through the thin glass transom window above the doors. His action took the seven remaining guards stationed outside by surprise. As he flew over them, they did their best to follow his movement with their weapons, but like most aliens, their shots came slow and several meters behind.

Landing softly on the brick walkway leading up to the entrance, Adam rolled once and came up on one knee. With the flash rifle married to his chin, he sent a stream of bolts into the guards, literally ripping them apart at their waists.

He then scanned the front of the building, his movements, and those of his rifle, acting as one. When he was satisfied there was no further movement in his direction, he slowly rose to his feet.

No one appeared to be left alive in the compound, or those who were chose to stay indoors and out of sight. It was a wise decision.

Calmly, Adam Cain snugged down his boonie hat and shouldered the rifle. Then he turned and walked casually down the long driveway and through the open gates of the compound, his back illuminated by the flickering light from the now fully-involved fire, as it quickly consumed the building behind him....

**The End
of this Special Preview of:**

Alien Assassin

by T.R. Harris

Go to **TheHumanChronicles.com** for more information about the series and to help contribute to future volumes.

Contact author **T.R. Harris** directly at
bytrharris@hotmail.com
He welcomes all comments, critiques and suggestions.

Pick up all the books in
The Human Chronicles Saga

The Human Chronicles Saga: Part One – 5 Books

Book 1 – *The Fringe Worlds*

Book 2 – *Alien Assassin*

Book 3 – *The War of Pawns*

Book 4 – *The Tactics of Revenge*

Book 5 – *The Legend of Earth*

The Human Chronicles Saga: Part Two

Book 1 – *Cain's Crusaders*

Made in the USA
Middletown, DE
20 September 2023